great dream of heaven

great dream of heaven

STORIES

SAM SHEPARD

Alfred A. Knopf   New York   2002

THIS IS A BORZOI BOOK
PUBLISHED BY ALFRED A. KNOPF

www.aaknopf.com

Knopf, Borzoi Books, and the colophon are registered trademarks
of Random House, Inc.

"An Unfair Question" was previously published in *The New Yorker.*

Library of Congress Cataloging-in-Publication Data
Shepard, Sam, [date]
Great dream of heaven : stories / Sam Shepard. — 1st ed.
p.   cm.
Contents: The remedy man — Coalinga $\frac{1}{2}$ way — Berlin Wall piece — Blinking
eye — Betty's cats — The door to women — Foreigners — Living the sign —
The company's interest — Concepción — It wasn't Proust — Convulsion —
An unfair question — A frightening seizure — Tinnitus — The stout of
heart — Great dream of heaven — All the trees are naked.
ISBN 0-375-40505-4 (hc. : alk. paper)
1. West (U.S.)—Social life and customs—Fiction. I. Title.
PS3569.H394 G74 2002
813'.54—dc21
2002070054

Manufactured in the United States of America
First Edition

FIC
SHEPARD
01/03

Jessica

People used to say that the blessed "would see heaven"; my wish would be to see the earth forever. —Peter Handke

Contents

Many thanks to:

Jesse

John

Wim

T Bone

Dan

Hannah

Shura

and Walker

great dream of heaven

THE REMEDY MAN

E.V. made no bones about it; he was not a horse whisperer by any stretch. He was a remedy man. He could fix bad horses, and when he fixed them they stayed fixed. That's all he laid claim to. We had one that needed to be turned around real bad. A five-year-old my dad had claimed off the low end of the fair circuit out in Sonoma, running for $1,200 tags. He was good-looking enough with a powerful hip and gaskin but his mind was the size of a chickpea. The one intolerable habit he had was setting back hard against his lead shank when tied to anything solid. The day he dragged down half the side of our pole barn on top of himself was the day we called E.V. He showed up at our place a week late in his usual beat-up outfit: a '54 Chevy half ton with Arizona plates and a one-horse trailer sporting bald tires and a flapping canvas top. He always parked his rig down on the flat bottom and hiked the steep gravel grade up to the house because he had no rearview mirrors to negotiate our hairpin turnaround. He didn't come to our place that often because most of the "knuckleheads" Dad was able to deal with himself, but when E.V. did pay us a visit I always got excited about it.

E.V. was a springy little man in his late fifties with an exaggerated limp from having his kneecap crushed in a shoeing accident when he was about my age; about fourteen. He climbed the hill in

3

steady jerks, his gray felt hat pointing straight down at the ground and bobbing with his gait. He had an old patched inner tube slung over one shoulder and a thick snow white cotton rope dangled from his left hand with the loose end looped through his horse-hair belt. I always thought he must have washed that rope regular in Ivory to keep it so white. It was the cleanest thing about him. When he got to the top he wasn't puffing or blowing like you'd think a man his age would be. He just arrived like he'd been air-dropped. "So, Mason, you shipped him off to the killer's yet?" He grinned at my dad so you could catch a glimpse of his few brown jagged teeth and the tiny gleaming diamonds for eyes that jumped right out at you through hooded slits; like Indian eyes except they were ice blue.

"Waitin' on you another week I'da cut his head off myself," my dad said, and there wasn't that much fun in his voice.

"Apologize, Mason, but I had me a couple errands to run, down in Oakdale."

"Errands my ass. You were off runnin' pussy is all." E.V. gave out with a high shrill squealing that was pure animal glee and me and my dad had to give in to laughing with him although my dad cut it off shorter than I felt was natural. We walked down to the round pen in back of the battered barn where we had the gelding trapped, and when E.V. caught sight of all the torn-down splintered timbers from the horse's tantrum he started to giggle again.

"Hope that claimer cost more'n them two-by-twelves, Mason." My dad didn't laugh this time. His voice came out with a nasty edge to it.

"Time you git done with him he won't be worth a smooth nickel anyhow." E.V. winked at me without my dad noticing and in that wink I understood there might be grown men in this world who actually get a spark out of life and somehow manage to dodge

4

the black hole my dad had fallen into. When we reached the round pen E.V. let the inner tube slip off his shoulder to the dry ground, propped one boot up on a rail, and peeked in at the problem horse.

"Stout enough, isn't he?"

"Stout in his damn mind," my dad grumbled. E.V. just hunched there for a long while, studying the gelding as he trotted in short nervous circles, blowing snot, tail high and his black-rimmed ears pricked in our direction.

"He's not all that dumb." E.V. grinned, keeping his eyes pinned to the horse's action. "He already suspects we've brought an idea for him. Tell you what, son—" He turned to me and as soon as his light eyes fixed on me it was as though a warm hand landed softly on my chest. There was a kindness there that surprised me how much I yearned toward it. "Take this old rubber tube over to that sycamore and wrap it around that big knobby branch. You see that branch?" He pointed to an arm of the huge tree that had always reminded me of human flesh. It was bone white and muscular with red strips of bark swirling down through the deep creases of the trunk like arteries. That tree had always spooked me for some reason, especially when I was little, trailing back through the brushy hills in pitch black. Its whiteness seemed to pop out at me and the very branch E.V. was pointing to was the part that scared me the most. More than once I'd swung a wide circle around it with my old dun mare, making sure it couldn't spring out and snatch me sideways off the saddle. I was a lot younger then, though, and I gradually talked my mind out of fixing on it that way. "Loop one end through like this here, so it cinches up tight against itself." E.V. demonstrated the pattern on his outstretched arm, then tossed the inner tube in my direction.

"Better let me handle that," my dad muttered as he moved in as though to pick up the tube, but E.V. stopped him short.

"Nah, you let him do it, Mason. I'm gonna need you here to keep this gate propped open. He can manage. Tie it up good and high now, son. We want it way above his head." I took off fast with the tube before my dad had a chance to consider twice. I had a feeling E.V. had just invented the business about needing my dad to prop the gate. I'd seen him maneuver horses through plenty of gates without anyone's help.

I had to climb the spooky tree in order to get the tube up high enough where E.V. wanted it, and by the time I got done looping and cinching it down I could see E.V. already had the gelding caught with that white rope of his. My dad was just standing there useless by the gate. I had a real clear view of things from up there and the air smelled like fresh dirt and eucalyptus. You could see far off into the tan, rolling hills where the yearling bulls were raising dust in a line down to the water tank. As E.V. passed through the gate of the round pen the gelding exploded, farting and bucking to beat all hell. E.V. let out with that same high-pitched squealing cackle of his, sank to his haunches, and jerked the gelding's head down hard with the rope. The next move he made was so quick I could hardly follow it. It was like he was dancing a jig and singing at the same time. He flipped that big rope up over the horse's rump so it slipped straight down to its outside hock, then ran hard against it, taking the gelding's hind leg right out from under him. That horse came crashing down on his rib cage with such a booming thump I thought I felt the big tree shake. E.V. was really squealing with delight now as the horse regained his feet and shook himself all over, looking like the sky had fallen in on him. "You see that?" E.V. hollered through his convulsions. "He never even saw that comin'!" My dad was brushing dirt off his ass, trying to act like it was all routine, but I could see the white flush of fear still drawn on his face. Even from way up high I could see that. Then E.V. did a funny thing. He walked right up to that horse's head and blew softly into each nostril while he gently rubbed under its neck right between the saucer-shaped jawbones. The horse seemed to almost nod asleep for a second, blinking and dropping his neck down a notch. "Now he feels kinda stupid. He thinks he mighta done that to himself, see? He's gonna think twice before he bumps and crow-hops through that gate agin." E.V. chuckled and ran his gnarly hand down the horse's shoulder. My dad caught sight of me still perched high up on the tree limb and yelled out with that kind of voice that wants everyone to know it's in charge of things.

"You git down offa there now! We don't want this horse to go off again."

"I'm gonna need him to tie the rope, Mason. Lest you wanna gimme a boost up there on yer shoulders." E.V. giggled again while my dad grit his teeth and glared at me. I think he was actually jealous I was getting all the action. I could feel it over all that distance to the ground; how cut off he was. E.V. led the horse over to the sycamore and tossed the free end of the rope up to me. I caught the fuzzy tip of it on the first pitch. "Feed it through that tube and fix yourself a double half hitch," he called up to me. "Do it slow and easy, now, so we don't git him worried." I followed his instructions and as I was cinching up the second loop I could see that gelding was getting himself ready for a real set-to. The muscles along his backbone rippled up like a bull snake and dark patches of sweat broke along his bowed neck. I could smell fear as strong as a dead rat in the feed bin. Fear both ways; animal and human. I could see that horse's eyeball roll back and catch me perched above him. I could see everything turned around, from his perspective, and suddenly I realized I was going to be riding the knobby branch while he unleashed his fury and tried to pull the whole damn tree down on top of himself. "Now, you just hang tight to that branch, son, 'cause this bugger is about ready to come apart." E.V.'s voice put the chill on me as I locked my arms and legs around the branch, monkey style. The gelding made one powerful, quick jerk, shaking his head like a lion, but the rubber tube snapped him right back to square one. The branch sprang a little, casting brown clusters of leaves down on my head. I blew sycamore dust out of my nose and watched the particles of it catch sunlight as they floated down to the horse's devilish ears. "You just ride her out, son!" E.V. cackled. "You're doin' just fine!" His voice caught me in that limbo where you know there's nothing on earth that can help you now; nothing can save you, you're caught in the grips. My dad's face was pure white but to this day I don't know if it was me he was scared for or just the plain violence of the moment. The gelding snorted and pawed dirt, trying to figure out the rubber band effect of the inner tube. I thought for sure I heard a deep growl come out of him, more like the sound a bull can make when it's cornered and got its blood up. Then I could see him fix his mind. A suicidal decision passed through him, right down the length of his spine as he stretched out and set all twelve hundred pounds of raw muscle against that gleaming white rope. It was a long, slow, suspended action as the inner tube pulled like taffy and turned from black to grayish blue. Little chips of rubber started to pop off it from the extreme tension and I watched them fly into the heat of the day as though I were sitting way outside any danger; as though I were watching gnats buzz the water from the bank of a river. The branch began to bow and creak beneath me and the whole world bent sideways for a long second. When it happened it was almost slow and lazy. My heart leveled out into simple waltz time as the branch heaved up in a long arc and I saw all four feet of that gelding come clear off the ground and the wide-open panic in that horse's eye when he realized he was actually flying. His flat blazed face slammed square into the trunk of that granite sycamore and it sounded like somebody'd dropped a side of beef onto cold pavement. The branch kept throbbing for a while with me strangling it and staring straight down at the crumpled heap of the horse, flat out cold beneath me, blood rushing from both nostrils. The fat pink tongue dangled loose like a dead trout and the panicky voice of my dad was cutting through from another planet: "You kilt the son'bitch! Goddammit, E.V., you went and kilt him!" E.V. was already straddling the horse's neck and working the rope free. He peeled the gelding's eyelids back and spit on both eyeballs, then blew again, hard this time, in each ear. The horse gave a little twitch of his head and E.V. danced back away from him, giggling like a kid as he coiled up his powerful rope. "He ain't dead, he's just dreamin'," E.V. chuckled. "Unhitch that rope up there, would ya, son? Pass it on down to me." I did like E.V. said and watched my dad stagger toward his fallen horse and peer down at him for any sign of life.

"Lookit that blood! Lookit that! That's a dead horse! That was gonna make me a nice saddle horse, now lookit. He's worse'n dog food."

"He'll be on his feet in two minutes," E.V. snickered. "And I guaran-damn-tee ya he'll ground-tie with a shoelace, this day forward."

"Well, I ain't payin' good money for this kind of a deal. I didn't hire you to slaughter the dang fool. I coulda done that myself." My dad stomped off back toward the house, leaving me still up the tree looking down at E.V.'s sweat-stained hat and the smashed horse breathing in long whistling gurgles. E.V. kept coiling the rope in loose loops and spoke to no one in particular.

"Horse is just like a human being. He's gotta know his limits. Once he finds that out he's a happy camper." The horse bolted up to his feet as though on cue and shook himself again, sending long cords of blood flying across E.V.'s rope. E.V. just smiled and held the rope out away from his chest. "I was gonna have to wash it anyhow." He stepped softly up to the horse's shoulder with that peculiar hitch in his walk and grabbed a shank of mane, then led the bay back toward the round pen. The gelding led right along beside him as quiet as an old broodmare. E.V. stopped down there beside the water tank and cleaned the horse's nose out, then gently rubbed its eyes with the cold water and turned him back loose in the round pen. He watched him for a while the same way he'd watched him before, one foot propped on the rail and twirling the tip of his cotton rope. Everything was silent. The light went on in my dad's bedroom. The wind shifted and rattled the tin on the good side of the hay barn.

Long after E.V. left and I heard the sound of his Chevy die away into the toolie-fog seeping up through the valley floor, I just stayed high up in that tree. I stayed and watched the night fall and the owls move into the tall eucalyptus and station themselves for the slightest hint of any skittering through the yard. I reached down and grabbed the open loop of the inner tube that E.V.'d left behind. I grabbed the black rubber with both hands and slid off the smooth muscle of the branch, bobbing in space, arms strung out tight above my head, spinning slowly in the cool night air. The whole ranch turned below me. I arched my head back and my mouth went open to the black sky. The giant splash of the Milky Way must have caused the high shrill squealing to burst out of me, just like someone had pulled a cord straight down my spine. My skin was laughing. I heard my dad come out on the screen porch and yell my name but I didn't answer. I just hung there spinning in silence. I knew right then where I'd come from and how far I'd be going away.

COALINGA ½ WAY

He pulls over at the edge of the Coalinga feedlots and kills the engine. He has a view of the entire yawning San Joaquin but he's in no state to take it in. He feels no awe or sense of history about it, only contempt. The scalding air stinks of cattle. His pulse pounds through the base of his dry tongue and his whole head is on fire. His entire head. There's the silent pay phone, marooned on a chrome pipe with a pale blue plastic globe guarding it from the blasting sun. Its modernism disgusts him; makes him feel worse off, more removed. Beyond the phone, pathetic groups of steers stand on tall black mounds of their own shit, waiting for slaughter. Heat vapors rise from the mounds, cooking under the intense sun as though about ready to explode and send dismembered cow parts flying into the highway. Beyond the cattle there's nothing. Absolutely nothing moves, clear to the smoky gray horizon.

"It's time to make the call!" It comes to him like a voice; a command. If he doesn't make it now, he never will. Dread or no dread, it's time to make the call. He swings out and slams the door of the Dodge. The sound doesn't carry. It ends abruptly at his feet. He digs for change and crunches toward the phone through loose gravel and mouse bones, flattened beer cans and sun-bleached condoms. He sees all these objects very clearly now; sees them as though

11

they've been laid out on a steel table for his personal examination, like crime evidence. He can see her face too. Her big eyes. He can hear her voice before he drops the quarter—the terror in it. He makes it person-to-person collect, negotiating through the composite voices of recorded operators; female voices, different ages, each one completely devoid of sexuality. He knows his wife has got to be home. He's timed it, knowing she'll be there. She is.

"Where are you?" is the first thing she says. He knew that would be the first thing and his dread cranks up a notch.

"Coalinga," he says.

"What're you doing way down there?"

"I'm on my way south."

"Why? What're you doing?"

"I'm just—going."

"Going? When are you coming back?" she says, and he can hear she knows already.

"I'm not."

"You mean, ever? You're not *ever* coming back?"

"I don't think so."

"Oh my God!" she gasps, and now he hears the horrible thud of shock in her chest; her breath chopping away into black silence. Nothing. A truck blasts by and drones off into the steel gray bands of heat. A single cow moans. His hearing has become acute. "Listen," she suddenly says. "Why don't I drive halfway down and meet you? You drive halfway back and I'll drive halfway down. Does that sound fair? Just to talk, okay? Will you do that? Will you meet me halfway?"

"I don't think so," he says, trying to keep his voice steady.

"It seems like after fifteen years we could just do that for each other. Just meet halfway. That's not too much to ask, is it? Then we could at least talk. We can't talk like this, on the phone."

"I've already come this far," he says.

"I know. That's what I'm saying. I'm not asking you to come back all the way. I'm willing to drive halfway down there and meet you somewhere."

"Where?" he says. "There's nothing down here."

"I don't know. Gilroy or something."

"Gilroy?"

"Anywhere! I don't care where it is. It doesn't matter."

"No, I can't go back," he says.

"Why not? After all this time? All these years? What about Spence? Are you going to tell him you're not coming back?"

"Not right now."

"When?" she says.

"I don't know."

"What am I supposed to tell him then?"

"Tell him I'll call him."

"When?"

"I'm not sure." Silence again. A high piercing shriek of a circling hawk. A Jeep roars past. A Jeep with no windows or doors, just the wind ripping across the wide-eyed face of the driver. "Are you still there?" he says to the phone.

"Where am I supposed to go?" she says.

"I don't know."

"Is this about her? Is that what this is? You're going down there to be with her?"

"Yeah. I am."

"What about *her* man? Isn't she with someone too?"

"Yeah."

"Well, what about him? What's she going to do?"

"She's going to tell him, I guess."

"She hasn't told him yet?"

"I don't know."

"You don't know and you're still going down there?"

"Yeah."

"You know what this is for me, don't you? I mean my history and everything—my father—"

"Yeah. I do."

"Your father too."

"Yeah."

"You didn't think of that?"

"I did."

"And Spence—" Her voice chokes. He stares down at his boots. He wants to feel something. He presses the heel of one boot down hard on the toe of the other. The sun cuts the back of his neck. "What is this going to do?" Her voice comes back and he can hear it's taking everything she has. "What is this going to change? Changing women. Do you think that's going to solve something;. make something different?"

"I don't know," he says.

"I mean whatever it is that's making you—that's causing this thing in you—It's inside *you,* isn't it? Swapping women isn't going to make that any different. That's not going to solve anything."

"No. Probably not."

"It didn't solve it when you changed over to me, did it?"

"No."

"How many times have you done this and what's it come to?"

"I don't know."

"So why are you doing it again?" He can't answer. He has no answer. The steers set up a long series of desperate bawling, then drop off into silence again. The heavy stench and the heat are making his eyes water. He rubs a sleeve across them and believes for a second that he's actually crying; believes the gesture is about some

14

kind of grief. He sees himself from a distance now, as though looking down from a great height, like the hawk's point of view: a tiny man in vast space, clutching a chunk of black plastic. He can't hear his breath now, he's so far away. He can't hear his heart.

"Tell Spence I'll call him, okay?" he says at last.

"You can't just do me a favor and meet me halfway?"

"I can't," he says.

"Are you going to call again?"

"Yes. I said I would."

"When?"

"Tomorrow."

"You've got to talk to Spence."

"I will."

"*I* can't tell him."

"I'll call."

"All right," she says, and hangs up with a soft click. He wishes she would have slammed the receiver down and yelled something. He wishes she would have screamed something he'd never heard before. Some word. He keeps clutching the phone and staring out at the acres of trapped cattle. He can't believe he's going through with this; can't believe it's done. He can't go back. He's more than halfway to L.A. now. He can't ever go back. A door has shut behind him with a soft click. Some woman's voice is speaking to him. A prerecorded operator voice instructing him to hang up the phone. It keeps repeating, then segues into sharp beeps. He drops the phone and lets it swing. The beeps continue.

He drives on and turns the air conditioner up high. His head starts cooling down some. His eyes have finished stinging and the stink of cattle fades slowly behind him. He tries to keep watching the swinging phone in the rearview mirror but loses it quickly, like some small part of himself left behind. The sharp beeps continue in the top of his skull. He remembers a conversation he had with his wife in his head, less than a month ago. His head was not on fire back then. He remembers this imaginary conversation took place on this very same highway, almost exactly halfway like he is now except then he was heading north. Then he was heading *back* to her. He was telling her how he'd never leave her; talking out loud in the truck as though she were right there beside him. Telling her how he'd come to a decision. How he'd never repeat his father's mistakes. He would never abandon his son. He was fervent about it—elated. He remembers the feeling of being full of conviction. The impression of himself as an honest man. The hot valley wind through the open window felt like a source of strength back then. He could hardly wait to tell her when he got back; when she'd come running down the front porch to greet him. But he never did. Something happened. Something shifted. Something he never saw taking place.

Night falls fast through the Tejon Pass and now he knows he's gone way past halfway. Now he knows he's deep inside the muscle of an action he'd only ever imagined himself doing. Now some scared boy takes the place of the man; shoves him over, grabs the wheel, hunches forward into the dark, and rides the snaking mountain down into the wild lights of L.A.

At the intersection of Highland and Sunset, huge billboards with shiny movie-star faces leer down at him. Some are in action; running from explosions, falling through white space, punching, shooting, crashing their way through plate-glass windows. Others are frozen in sweaty clinches, mouths agape, necks arched back; transcended through orgasm to plateaus of ecstasy beyond the common man. Stretch limos with tinted windows and thumping, subsonic bass lines haunt the streets with secret cargo. Coveys of hysterical, screaming girls, hair teased, tattooed and pierced in every department, run toward a nightclub framed in pulsing lavender neon, stumbling in their elevator-high platforms only to wait in line while bald bouncers frisk them.

He checks into the Tropicana with no bag, no toothbrush, no change of underwear. The night clerk has junkie eyes. Eyes that could care less what or who stands across from him. His room has nothing but a bed and a phone. It smells like bad Chinese food. He slashes open the green plastic curtains and stares out at the rippling reflections of light off the pool. The hotel logo, a red neon palm tree, dances its reflection in the deep end. A fat man wearing a black Speedo sits perched at the top of the water slide, staring down at his toes. He wriggles them as though testing for signs of life. A TV goes on in a room across the pool deck. Someone pulls their curtains shut.

He turns back into his room and snaps the light on. He goes to the phone. He has the number memorized. He's called this number maybe a million times from every conceivable dark corner over the past two years. He's gripped phones in every possible emotional state, awaiting the voice on the other end. The voice he's become convinced he can't live without. The voice he's given everything up for.

"Hello," the voice says, and he can't believe it's so simple.

"It's me," he says. She laughs and he feels a rush of white excitement like falling high from a rope swing into icy water.

"Where are you?" she giggles.

"I'm here. I'm right here."

"In town?"

"Yeah. I'm at the Tropicana."

"The Tropicana!" she squeals. "What're you doing there?"

"I've left."

"What?" she says, and stops laughing.

17

"I've left."

"Not— Your wife you mean?"

"Yeah."

"You told her?"

"Yeah. I did. I told her." She laughs again but it's different now. It has a guarded edge to it.

"Well—" she says. "So she knows all about it then?"

"Yeah. She does."

"What'd you tell her?"

"I told her I was leaving."

"When did this happen?"

"Today," he says. "Just today. I drove all the way down here."

"That's crazy!" she says, and laughs again, but this time it hardly sounds like a laugh at all. It sounds worried.

"Can you come over?" he says. "I need to see you."

"What? Now, you mean? Right now?"

"Yeah. Come on over. I'm in number seventeen."

"Well, I can't right now. There's—I just can't."

"Why not?" he says.

"I'm—well, actually I was just getting ready to leave."

"Where are you going?"

"Indiana. David's got a new commission out there."

"David?" he says.

"Yes. It just came up. He's waiting for me."

"Waiting for you where?"

"In Indiana. I just told you."

"You're flying out to Indiana to meet David?"

"Yes. I was just going out the door when the phone rang." He hears the loud splash of the fat man hitting the pool outside. Then nothing. A distant siren. "Hello," she says. "Are you still there?"

"Where am I supposed to go?" he says.

18

BERLIN WALL PIECE

My dad knows absolutely nothing about the eighties. I have to
interview him for my seventh-grade social studies class and he
knows nothing. He says he can't remember anything about the cars
or the hair or the clothes or the music or anything. He says the
economy sucked and that was a Republican thing but other than
that nothing stands out for him. He says the most significant thing
about the eighties was that was when he first met my mother and
when me and my sister were both born. Those two things. That's
it. When I tell him it's not supposed to be about personal stuff he
says what else is there? I tell him I need stuff about style and fads
and what was going on in the country at the time and he says none
of that has anything to do with reality; that reality is an "internal
affair" and all the rest of that stuff is just superficial and a lie—like
the news. He says the news is all lies and the reason it's so popular
is that it sells itself as all truth and people believe it because they'd
rather believe in a lie. The truth is too much for them to swallow.
That's what he says. I tell him this is just supposed to be a simple assignment thing about the decade of the eighties, not about
"reality" and the "news," but he says you can't exclude the question
of reality; that the question of reality supersedes all the other questions about hair and cars and music and things like that. Then he

says he can't even remember living through the eighties and that maybe he wasn't even alive back then, but then he had to have been he says because he remembers meeting my mother, and me and my sister were both born back then. He repeats that. My dad's fucking crazy. He is. I didn't realize it for a long time but he is. My sister knows more about the eighties than my dad does and she's only a year or so older than me. She's in the ninth grade. She knows all kinds of things—don't ask me how—like the way they used to wear their pants back then in this weird tapered style where they actually folded the pant leg inside their zip-up boots and the girls wore ripped up fishnet stockings and cheap white cotton gloves trying to imitate Madonna, who I guess was the bomb in music back then, or Michael Jackson, who'd just started bleaching his black skin, or Bob Seger, who I thought was only known for that dumb "Like a Rock" Chevy commercial. Then, on top of that, she knows all kinds of political stuff like Russia not being Russia anymore and the Berlin Wall coming down, and I ask her how she knows things like that and she says because she was there. "Yeah, right," I say, and she says, "Yeah, I can prove it," and she runs upstairs to her bedroom and comes back down with a chunk of painted concrete about the size of a cheeseburger and sets it down on the kitchen counter right in front of me and my dad. "What's that?" I say, and she says, "That's a piece of the Berlin Wall."

"It is!" my dad says, and gets very excited about it. "That's exactly what that is! Isn't that incredible?" He picks it up and turns it over, feeling the weight of it as though it might be from another planet or something. "When did you go to the Berlin Wall, honey?" My sister looks at him, dumbfounded.

"Don't you remember?" my sister says. "I went with Mom and Aunt Amy."

"I don't remember that," my dad says. "How old were you?"

He remembers nothing. Like he's losing his mind. How could he not remember something like that? His own daughter going to the Berlin Wall. He's not that old to be losing his mind but he is.

"Where was I?" my dad says.

"You must've stayed home," my sister says.

"I must have," he says.

I ask my sister how she got a piece of the Berlin Wall and she says they were driving through Berlin at the time they were tearing the wall down and the workers were just giving away pieces of it, handing it through the car windows. She says it was like a party. She was three years old and these big hands of hairy men were coming through the windows handing them chunks of rock and concrete as though it were cake and she had no idea what it was all about. I'm staring at the chunk of cement on the kitchen counter. One side is smooth and flat and painted flashy turquoise and purple with a skinny yellow stripe cutting down the middle—it looks like spray paint, maybe graffiti. The other side is broken and rough and you can see the fragments of things that they made the concrete out of: small smooth stones that look like they could have come out of somewhere deep in the woods and sharp gravel mixed in with this chalky-looking cement that doesn't look American at all and then these tiny glittering particles. When you run your finger along the edge of it, it makes the sound of glass more than stone. My sister offers to let me take the piece of the Berlin Wall to school and show it around in my class, which is a very generous offer for her, I think. Then my dad picks up the heavy chunk of the Berlin Wall and drops it into a Ziploc bag and when I ask him why he's doing that he says so it doesn't get lost. He says it's very important that it doesn't get lost or stolen because it's a real live piece of modern history. What does he care? He's not even sure he was alive back then and now he's calling this piece of concrete alive. He's not making any sense at all. He takes out a big roll of silver plumber's tape from a drawer and tears a piece off with his teeth. He sticks the strip of tape on the Ziploc bag and then takes a black Magic Marker and writes "BERLIN WALL PIECE" like it's some kind of museum label or something. "There," he says, "that oughta do it." He's totally nuts.

My sister's doing her homework all this time but keeps coming up with other stuff about the eighties and fires it at me as she's working as though her mind is able to split right down the middle and do two things at once. She's totally brilliant, I think. "There was some volcano out west in Washington that erupted," she says. "It erupted and kept right on erupting off and on for the rest of the year. That was in the eighties, wasn't it, Dad?" I don't know why she's asking him. How would he know?

"I don't know," my dad says as he wipes black ants off the counter with a wet sponge. He doesn't try to step on them, he just wipes them onto the floor and lets them crawl away.

"Why don't you kill them," I ask my dad.

"I like ants," he says. "They remind me of summer and hot places. We always had ants when I was growing up." He says this as though he were talking about puppies or guinea pigs.

"And they discovered AIDS!" my sister blurts out. "That's when they first discovered the AIDS virus, was the eighties." She's on a roll now. I don't know how her mind works. It's a mystery to me; like she can scroll stuff up like she's looking at it on a green screen or something. AIDS? Where does she come up with that off the top of her head? "And Marvin Gaye got shot by his father, didn't he?" she says. Suddenly my dad stops cold in the middle of the kitchen like he's been hit in the back of the head by a board or something.

"That's right," my dad says. "I remember that."

"You do?" I say, and I'm looking straight at him, standing there with the sponge hanging down from his hand dripping on the floor and he's staring out across the kitchen without seeing me or my sister or anything but as though he's trying to nail down this picture of Marvin Gaye in his mind all shot in the head and bloody from some picture in the news back then that he hates.

"I remember that very clearly," he says. "I was in California. It was 1984—the summer or spring of 1984 and it was very hot. Marvin Gaye was killed by his father and his father was a reverend, wasn't he? I think he was. A man of the church and he shot his son in the head over something—over something to do with women, I think. Something about a woman, wasn't it?" He turns to my sister, who doesn't realize he's asking her a direct question and just continues on with her head down in her book, working hard on her homework. "Wasn't it something to do with a woman?" he says to her again. My sister finally looks up at him and sees that he's talking to her. She stares at him but you can see she's thinking about some math problem.

"I don't know, Dad," she says, and her eyes go back down into her books. He looks at me, sort of searching for a second. I don't know the answer. How am I supposed to know the answer? I wasn't even born yet when that happened. He looks out across the kitchen again, toward the dark windows.

"Huh, it's funny I'd remember that," he says and then he tosses the sponge into the sink and walks out onto the screen porch and stands there for a long while looking out at the lawn and the maple tree. Spring peepers are chirping from the pond down the hill. I pick up the Ziploc bag with the piece of the Berlin Wall inside and hold it up to the light. It's just a chunk of concrete.

"Don't lose that," my sister says without looking up.

"How can I lose it?" I say. "It's labeled."

BLINKING EYE

She's the youngest daughter of the woman whose ashes rest on the seat beside her in a dark green ceramic urn. She feels good about being the youngest and the one with sole responsibility for driving her mother's remains clear across the country in time for the family funeral in Green Bay. She's glad she finally has this time alone with her mother and she speaks to the tall green urn, as she barrels across Utah, in a voice exactly like the one she used when her mother was living. She speaks out loud while her bright eyes scan the enormous white sea of salt.

"I don't know, Mom—I thought that check was for me. I mean, I honestly did. I never would've cashed it otherwise. Now Sally's all pissed—outraged, like I've stolen something from her, committed some horrible crime behind her back. She gets so violent with me sometimes. You've never seen her get like that but she does. She never acts like that around you, but with me it's a whole 'nother story. See, I thought you told me to go ahead and cash that check. That was my understanding. I thought you told me to go ahead and take it once this whole thing was finished. I mean, not like you owed it to me or anything. I never expected that. I just thought it was something you wanted me to have. It was just sitting there, plain as day, on your table, made out to cash, so I took it. Now

24

Sally's saying I should have split it with her down the middle. I mean it was only a hundred bucks and she's acting like— Oh well— It doesn't matter. I don't want to sound like— I just can't believe her sometimes. Like I'm her worst enemy or something. Now she's going to be out there at the funeral and I've got to go through this whole thing all over again with her. This whole routine. She won't give it up. I mean, I'd be glad to give her the entire hundred bucks if it means so much to her. I would. I don't give a shit about the hundred bucks. I really don't. Except I used it for the car payment and that's what she thinks, see— She thinks I was desperate and just went ahead and cashed the check without consulting her about it. That's what gets her. That I never consulted her. She thinks—"

Just then, she sees something on the long ribbon of empty road up ahead; something fluttering, hovering low over the broken white divider line. Her mind tries to fit the shape and action to something known: a busted cardboard box flapping; a piece of someone's clothing; a chunk of shredded truck tire. She lets up on the gas and drops all connection with her dead mother or her living pissed-off sister. She's in her body now. She thinks it might be feathers; a red-tipped wing rising, then slapping back down to the pitted asphalt. A giant bird! She's almost on top of it now, mashing the brake and swerving off onto the shoulder. She sees a piercing yellow eye as she passes. A scared eye buried in a tangle of blood and feathers pasted to the blacktop, the enormous wing thrashing to get airborne. "My God, it's a hawk!" she says out loud. "A beautiful hawk! Oh my God! Oh my God, what am I going to do?" She jumps out and slams the door, then runs toward the wounded bird through the chalky dust the car has kicked up. She stops short and cradles her open jaw with both palms, a gesture she's picked up from too much daytime television. She coughs from the dust and starts repeating "Oh my God! Oh my God! Oh my God!" as though it were a mantra that might somehow deliver her from the situation. The huge hawk keeps screaming and beating itself to death in the middle of the road. She looks up and down the highway but there's not a car in sight. The heat coming off the asphalt is already broiling the crepe soles of her tennis shoes as she hops from one foot to the other. She inches in closer to the bird, still clutching her face with both hands and taking little mincing baby steps like she's afraid she might fall into a deep hole. She tries to speak to the hawk in a voice she used to use on puppies and painted turtles. "Oh, you poor baby. You poor little thing. It's all right. It's going to be all right. It's a terrible, terrible thing." The hawk settles down for a second, smoothing its neck feathers, as though it finds something soothing in the voice; as though it were actually listening. Its torn chest is throbbing. The yellow eye blinks mechanically. The head cranes back over itself and then the whole bird explodes again into wild flailing and high shrieks, blood shooting in strings across the blank sky.

She runs back to the car and yanks her sweatshirt out of the back seat. It's her high school track sweatshirt with "MUSTANGS" printed in blue across the chest and a wild horse galloping, mane and tail flagging out through imaginary prairie wind. Again, she looks up and down the highway but there's nothing, only the weird steely heat rays rising off the salt flats; a single seagull gliding south. She moves toward the hawk, holding the sweatshirt out in front of her like a matador warily testing a yearling bull. She's not sure how she's going to attempt the capture; whether to throw the sweatshirt over the dying bird or just tackle him straight on and wrap him up fast. She has no experience with hawks. She starts repeating "Oh my God" again but stops herself this time, hearing how pathetic and hopeless it sounds in the endless space. She tries her puppy voice again but gives up on that too and settles for silence. The silence scares her to the bone; scares her worse than the shrieking hawk and the wind moaning across the treeless flats. She moves in closer and sees that the bird has really been mangled badly across its whole left side. "A car must have smacked him as he rose up out of the ditch," she thinks. "Why wouldn't somebody stop? You'd think they'd stop if they hit a bird like that. Such an incredible bird. I mean, it's not like hitting a crow or a sparrow or something. This is a hawk! Look at this hawk! He's huge! He's amazing! Look at his eye!" She's never been so close to a hawk before. "I can't believe it," she whispers. "You're so pretty. You are the prettiest thing I've ever seen in my whole life. You are a gorgeous hawk. Oh, don't do that! Don't do that! Please don't do that!" she says as the hawk goes into another seizure, smashing away with its one good wing. She darts in fast and tries to catch hold of the giant wing with the sleeve of her sweatshirt but the hawk slashes out with beak and talons, making a horrible hissing sound. She backs off and has a sudden urge to fall to her knees and break down. She wants to break down badly. She wants to fold up completely and have this all disappear. She dances in tight circles in the middle of the empty highway; jumping and slapping her thighs with the sweatshirt. "Oh God! Oh God! Oh God!" she cries out. Nothing answers. She stops still. The hawk stops too and just stares at her with his blinking yellow eye, the black pupil cold as stone in the center. His beak is wide open, panting for air. She can see his pink wedge of a tongue. She hears it clicking against the back of his throat. "Let me just take you, okay?" she pleads softly. "Let me just wrap you up and take you away. I'll find someone to make you all better. Someone to fix you up. All right?" The bird just blinks. His head snaps from side to side, bewildered. "I promise I won't hurt you. I promise. I just want to save you, that's all. Don't you want to be saved?" The bird lets out a different tone, a lower crackling kind of sound, then lets his neck fall back on his damaged wing. His leg twitches and his good wing spreads out flat across the white line of the road like some exotic Japanese fan. "Oh, don't die!" she tells him. "Please don't die. I couldn't stand that. I don't want you to die!" She leaps for the bird and pins him down with the sweatshirt. She's surprised how easy it is. The hawk hardly protests. He rolls his head around, feathers bristled, and arches his gaping mouth toward her chin. The hissing sound comes again. She flips him over and ties the sleeves of the sweatshirt tight across his chest. There's blood smeared all over her hands and arms now. It has a wild smell to it. Wilder than human blood; like rusting metal. She runs for the car, carrying the hawk across her belly. A truck appears from out of nowhere but she can't drop the bird to wave to it. She twists in a tight circle, tracking the truck with her desperate eyes as it flashes past, heading for Winnemucca. She sees the driver clearly. He's looking straight at her from high up in his cab. He sees a girl clutching a bloody sweatshirt, screaming with panic. She sees a blond beard, blue eyes, and a black ski cap pulled down tight over his ears. She's yelling "Stop! Stop! Please stop!" and it looks, for a second, like he will. The truck jerks down and starts to pull off to the side. The jake brakes hiss and blow steam. One of the back tires locks up screeching. She smells the burning rubber. Then, before she can even begin to feel relief, the truck accelerates and bolts back onto the highway. "Wait!" she screams, but he's already cranking through the gears; gone in a long plume of white dust that sparkles blue and gold in the glaring sun. The hawk thumps her in the belly with his one strong leg. She gets him to the car and sets him gently on the back seat, checking the knot again across his chest and asking him please to hold on, not to die; she'll find help and everything will be all right. Somehow some miracle is bound to take place.

She drives on toward Salt Lake, talking to the hawk in a voice she used to use with her little brother whenever he got in trouble; whenever he'd done something her father wasn't supposed to know about. The hawk never stops blinking. She tilts the rearview mirror so she can see its yellow eye. Her arm reaches out dreamily and her fingers lightly caress the cold green ceramic urn. Her body calms down and she begins to feel a strange tranquillity with the idea that she alone is responsible for the wounded and the dead. She feels confident now that she can see this thing through, no matter what the outcome. She snaps the radio on to an oldies channel: Clyde McPhatter singing "A Lover's Question" in high pristine falsetto. The voice melts through her and seems to be having the same salving effect on the hawk. She can't believe how still he is. She has no idea where she's going to find help for an injured hawk but, somehow, she's not worried. The panic has left her. She keeps hunching up on the steering wheel now and then; checking in the mirror; watching the blinking eye to make sure it hasn't died. She thinks of her sister Sally again and the hundred bucks. It just comes back to her like a bad habit. She thinks of Wisconsin and all those relatives awaiting her mother's ashes. She starts seeing their faces: aunts and uncles, cousins she's lost track of, kids she doesn't know how she's related to. She drifts into visions of the funeral; weeping faces, Bible verses, someone singing.

The hawk suddenly goes completely berserk and busts out of its sweatshirt bondage, shrieking like a banshee. She turns back quickly to see him plastered up against the rear window, both wings stretched to their limit; frozen like some medieval gargoyle. The car lurches onto the shoulder then hits the ditch, pitching the dark green ceramic urn to the floor. Ashes spew across the dashboard and windshield. A cloud envelops the upholstery. She's breathing it in as she clutches wildly at the spinning wheel. Her mother has entered her lungs. The hawk tumbles forward, black talons stretched taut, clutching the air and entangling itself in her long red hair. She screams in exactly the same pitch as Clyde McPhatter. The car jolts to a stop in a sand dune but the engine keeps running. "A Lover's Question" keeps playing. She hurtles backward out of the car with the hawk still snared in her hair. She pummels its bloody body with her small white fists, rolling in the sand as though trying to extinguish a sudden fire. The hawk breaks free and flies off like it had never been wounded, both wings pumping, then gliding downward and churning again to gain altitude. She watches it from the sand as it floats away. The radio keeps playing. The engine keeps humming. Wind moans across the low, empty expanse. She stays there on her belly for a long, long time until her breath comes back. Her face is coated with ashes. She can feel them clinging to her lips as she runs her tongue across them. Her mother tastes like salt.

It takes her three more days to reach Green Bay, and by the time she gets there, the hawk has left her mind completely. The streets are draped in green and gold banners. Snowbanks stained with mud and diesel fuel; Dairy Queens, Taxidermy, Cheese Factories, Packers paraphernalia is on sale at greatly reduced prices. She hunts for the address of her aunt Dottie. She remembers some of these streets from when she was a very little girl. She remembers her mother pulling her and her sister around in a red wagon with wooden slats built up on the sides so the two of them wouldn't tumble out. She barely remembers her father at all. She runs her fingers down the silky neck of the dark green urn, thinking it will be the last time she'll have her mother all to herself. She checks the lid to make sure it's tight. She managed to collect most of the spilled ashes by scraping them into her tennis shoe and pouring them gently back in, but tiny flakes of her mother still cling to the rubber floor mats, the dashboard, and some must have surely blown out forever into the vast white Utah wasteland. "They'll never know the difference," she thinks. "They'll never know she's not all in there." She spots her aunt's house and turns into the narrow driveway, thinking it all looks much smaller than she remembered. Her heart starts racing for some reason, like she's got something to be guilty about. Her sister Sally's there to meet her, standing right there by the porch like she's been expecting her any minute. No one else, just Sally. She cuts the engine and grabs the dark green urn with both hands, bearing down on the slender neck; praying she won't drop it. Sally opens the car door for her and takes the urn from her sister, feeling the sudden weight of their mother between them. The sisters smile at each other, then Sally says: "Did you bring my hundred bucks?"

BETTY'S CATS

Now Betty, how are we going to address this situation?

What's the problem?

The cats, Betty.

That's not *my* problem.

It's *our* problem, Betty. They're going to confiscate your trailer again if you don't do something about it.

They can't confiscate my trailer.

They did it once already.

Well, they won't do it again.

Betty— They've given you notice. If you don't get rid of the cats they're going to take your trailer away. It's as simple as that. Now I don't want to see that happen again. I mean where are you going to go, Betty?

I'll find something.

I'm willing to help you out, Betty, but I have to have your cooperation.

You don't have to help.

I *want* to help.

That's not my main problem. I'll tell you what my main problem is.

What's your problem, Betty?

The Health Department. That's my problem.

They're just doing their job. They get complaints because of the smell. They have to come over there.

They don't have to come over.

It's part of their job. They have to respond to complaints like that. I mean, I was over there the other day with Lois and as soon as she stepped out of the car she said, "What's that smell?" and I said, "That's Betty's cats."

Lois?

That's what she said. The minute she stepped out of the car.

Lois was over there?

She came with me.

Lois hates those cats.

That's not true, Betty.

She hates *my* cats.

That's not true. She could smell it, that's all.

Could *you* smell it?

Anybody can smell it.

That's the cats.

I *know* that's the cats. That's what I'm saying. Now what are we going to do about it?

Well, I'm not getting rid of them.

Then we have to clean it up. That's all there is to it. Now, I'm willing to come over there and help you, Betty, but you've got to go along with it. I mean last time I was over there cleaning up, that gray cat kept following me around doing his business right behind me. Now, that's not right, Betty.

Cricket?

That gray one. I don't know his name. He's got no hair.

That's Cricket.

What happened to his hair?

He was born like that.

Is there something wrong with him?

There's nothing wrong with Cricket.

Well, if he's not right you should get rid of him.

There's nothing wrong with him.

Well, I've never seen a hairless cat before.

That's the way he was born.

All right, but we have to address this, Betty.

I *am* addressing it.

No you're not, Betty. They keep giving you warnings and notices and nothing gets done.

I've got other problems.

What other problems?

The trailer's not level. I need six piers.

Piers?

Those metal piers to jack the trailer up; get it level. I need six of them.

I don't know anything about motor homes. I've never had one.

Well, that's what I need. Someone's gotta climb underneath there and set those piers. I can't do it by myself.

Well, maybe we can find someone over at the trailer court.

I can't do it. It needs two.

I'm sure we can find someone to help you with that but that's not really the issue.

That *is* the issue.

No it's not, Betty.

What's the issue then?

The cats, Betty!

I can't live in an unlevel trailer. It throws everything off.

What are we going to do about the cats!

I'm not locking them up. That's for sure.

Well, they can't have the run of the whole trailer.

Why not?

Because you can't control them! They do their business all over the place.

I don't *want* to control them.

Then you'll have to get rid of them.

I'm not getting rid of them either.

Then they're just going to come and take your trailer again. That's all there is to it.

Let them take it.

What will you do? Where are you going to go?

I'll find something.

Me and Lois can't take you. There's just no room.

I'm not living with Lois.

Now Betty, she's helped you out a lot. You know that.

When?

She's been over there doing the same thing I was doing.

What was that?

Cleaning up, Betty. Cleaning up after the cats. She had the whole place done for you once. She put up a partition, a board, back by the kitchenette. She had that piece of plywood set up and all the cats were back in there and the first thing you did when you got back was you took the board down.

They can't live like that. Trapped in the kitchen.

They weren't trapped. They had plenty of room.

They were trapped. Lois hates those cats.

Oh, Betty—

What?

I don't know. It's either that or get rid of them.

I'm not getting rid of them.

You could get rid of *some* of them.

Which ones?

That gray one for instance.

Cricket?

Yes, Cricket. The hairless one.

38

You don't like Cricket, do you?

It's not a question of liking or—

He was born like that.

I know he was born like that!

You can't blame him for that.

I'm not *blaming* him.

You said get rid of him.

I was just saying—if you wanted to get rid of some of them you could start with that one, since he's got no hair.

There's nothing wrong with him. He's just different.

He's got something. That's not natural, for a cat to have no hair.

He's never had hair.

Is it mange or something?

Mange is when the hair falls out. He's never had any hair to fall out.

Well, it's not healthy to keep a cat like that.

I'm not getting rid of Cricket.

Well, how about some of the other ones then. That orange one.

Which orange one?

That one with the funny stripe down his face.

Badger?

Is that his name? I don't know.

Badger's the daddy.

You ought to at least have him neutered then.

I'm not neutering Badger. He's the daddy.

Then you're just going to keep having more and more litters, Betty.

Well I can't stop them from having litters if they want to.

That's what neutering is for.

What?

To stop them from having more litters!

Well, I'm not doing that.

All right. I don't know—

What.

I don't know what we're going to do.

There's nothing to do.

I've tried to help you. Me and Lois both.

You can't help me.

Well we can't help you if you can't help yourself.

That's right. Nobody can help me.

So what are we going to do, Betty?

Nothing.

You're just going to let them take your trailer away again?

They can have it. It's a piece of shit anyway. It's never been level.

Well, you've let it get that way.

I can't ever remember it being level. It's always been a piece of shit.

It was level when you moved in there. And it was clean too. It got that way from those cats.

Yeah, I guess.

You know it's true.

Yeah. I know.

So what in the world are we going to do, Betty?

Nothing. There's nothing to do.

THE DOOR TO WOMEN

By this time, every last woman had been driven from the house—some by betrayal, most by neglect. There was only the boy and his grandfather left. They liked it that way. It was peaceful.

The boy was trimming the old man's toenails with the scissor accessory on his Swiss Army Knife. Brittle chunks of yellow nail popped over the boy's head and landed on the parquet floor of the tiny living room. The grandfather sat in his favorite Mission-style oak chair with the Daily Racing Form spread neatly across his lap, a Pall Mall burning in the stand-up ashtray beside him. The click of the nail chips landing on the polished wood, a lone mockingbird outside the window, and the old man's raspy breath were the only sounds. The boy kept working methodically, careful not to trim the corners of the nails too closely. He'd made that mistake once before and his grandfather came up lame for a week, necessitating long soaks in Epsom salts and apple vinegar. The grandfather never complained but the boy had to endure days of no words when the old man just seemed to drop deeper and deeper inside himself until, suddenly, one morning he sprang out of his chair, walked barefoot straight down to the Russian River, and waded in up to his chest. After that his toes were fine and he began talking again in his usual enthusiastic sprees. Now he's fully recovered. His toes are glowing like healthy night crawlers. He reaches for his red Bic pen and circles the name of a horse he likes in the eighth—"Monkish," a brown gelding shipping up from Pomona. In the blank column beside the name he scribbles "diminishing lengths—closes—just missed last out going 1 and ⅛." He caps the pen and returns it to his shirt pocket, then reaches for his Pall Mall. "This is the way it's supposed to be," he thinks, as he nestles his spine against the firm back of the chair; the way he's always imagined. There is no gap between his imagining and the way things are. He speaks softly to the boy kneeling at his gnarly feet. "Last week—when was it? When was that last week when we walked to supper down there by the river? You remember—it was coming dusk, I think."

"Oh, down at the Inn, you mean?" the boy answers, continuing with his work.

"That's it! 'The Inn.' Simple name like that. Think I could remember something simple like that."

"Yeah—'The Inn.' That's what they call it."

"Good food as I remember. Crispy duck. What is that? Some kind of Chinese deal, 'crispy duck'?"

"You like that. You always have that."

"You had your usual tuna melt."

"I did?" the boy says.

"Don't *you* start gettin' forgetful on me now. We don't need the both of us in the same jackpot."

"No, I remember. I always have the tuna melt."

"There ya go— And there was a girl down there. She seemed to know you. Who was that girl down there?"

"What girl's that, Grandpa?"

"That girl! Black hair. Magnificent eyes! She was our waitress."

"Oh—"

"You know the one I mean. Don't play dumb with me."

"Yeah. I've seen her before. She comes into the feed store a lot."

"Oh, she does, huh? So you *do* know her then?"

"Only from the feed store."

"She seemed to like you very much. Did you notice that?"

"No, not really," the boy says, and tucks his chin toward his chest as he works the long, spade-shaped middle toe.

"It's important to notice things like that. Don't let that type a thing slip through the cracks. Something like that could change your whole entire life. A moment like that."

"A moment like what?"

"Seeing that she liked you! The way she kept coming around to our table to pour us more water even when the glasses were full. She couldn't take her eyes off you."

"I don't know."

"You didn't notice that she kept coming around?"

"She was our waitress. She's supposed to come around."

"Not when the glasses are full! She didn't need to keep coming around like that."

"Well I didn't notice," the boy says with a note of finality, hoping to turn the subject. There is a sweet pause where the dove can be heard rustling in the dust of the road and the irrigation sweeps the cut pasture next door.

"Do you know her name?" the grandfather asks softly.

"No— It's Mexican or something— Something like 'Mina.' "

"Mina?"

"Something like that. She comes into the store all the time to get stuff for her goats."

"She keeps goats? A girl like that?"

"Yeah, what's wrong with that?" the boy says, and doesn't understand this feeling that surges up in him of wanting to defend the girl.

"Nothing. There's nothing wrong with that. I like a girl who can tend to livestock."

"I sweep up the oat dust and leftover alfalfa from the square bales and give it to her in empty feed sacks out back. Doesn't cost her a thing."

"Oh, so you do her favors then?"

"Well, just once in a while."

"She's very lovely, that one. Never seen eyes quite like that. Beyond her age, I'd say."

"I don't know how old she is."

"Difficult to say on a girl like that. Closer to being a woman."

"I don't know," the boy mumbles.

"Why would she keep goats? She's a waitress, isn't she?"

"She's probably got more than one job."

"Well, why would she keep goats?"

"I don't know. Maybe her parents. She's from a big family I think. She never says anything when she comes in. Just stands there and stares at me while I'm sweeping."

"She likes you."

"I don't know."

"Well, of course she does. What do you think she's staring at? The broom?"

"I don't know if she likes me, though. Just because she's staring."

"She likes you, believe me. You ought to be able to tell something like that by now. You're old enough."

The boy returns to the final toe on the old man's left foot. The little toe, the ugliest one, which is why he always saves it for last. The nail sticks up abruptly like a little shark tooth and he's never quite sure which angle to approach it from. He's afraid it might, somehow, leap out and bite him on the hand. The grandfather takes a long delicious pull on his cigarette and allows the smoke to very slowly creep out through his hairy nostrils and the dark corners of his mouth. He stares down at the crown of his grandson's bright head. He admires the structure of the skull, the perfect arch of the cranium, and inwardly congratulates himself on the boy's very masculine genealogy. "Of course the women are crazy about him. How could they resist!"

"I was thinking . . . ," the old man starts, then clears his throat and winces slightly at the final snap of the little silver scissors. "I was thinking it's been quite some time since we've had any women around the place." The boy finishes his job and blows any remaining clippings off the ancient toes. He stands slowly, folding the knife and returning it to his pocket. His eyes stay focused on the good job he's done. "I mean, when was it exactly your mother finally pulled up stakes? She was the last to go, wasn't she? After both your sisters. When was that?"

"I don't know," the boy answers, his eyes still fixed on his grandfather's toes.

"Year or more at least. Had to have been."

"Maybe. I can't remember."

"At least a year. I remember it was hotter than bloody blue Jesus. Mid-August. Must've been."

"Could be."

"We'd finished raking the almonds. I remember that much. All the Mexicans got paid off. That was a good bunch. Straight up from Sonora."

"I guess."

"She'd just finished pulling that dirty trick on your old man. Remember that? Not that he didn't deserve it."

"Who, Mom?"

"Yes. Don't you remember that one? Oh, that was a classic!"

The grandfather chuckles and clears his throat again. "That beat the cake! Right after that little flood we had down there in the basement. Rained for five days straight. Remember? River rose so bad they had to close down the old bridge. All your father's stuff was down there in the basement floating around in two foot of green slime."

"Oh yeah."

"We sump-pumped it the hell outta there but all his stuff kept laying around on the floor, gathering mildew. Looked like a damn disaster zone down there. Clothes stretched out like dead bodies. His fishing gear, old leather jackets, Indian saddle blankets; everything stinking and rotten. Musta laid down there a good three months or so just moldering away."

"Yeah, I remember the stink. You couldn't open the door or you'd get it in the face."

"That's it. Well, your mother—bless her heart—she, one day, took it into her head to scoop the whole mess up with a snow shovel and stuff it into boxes. Friend of hers helped her—that 'Kitty' or whoever she was; worked down at the Kmart by the highway there. She came over and helped. She's the one who brought the boxes. Two of 'em got plowed to the gills on cheap vodka and Kool-Aid, giggling their damn heads off and playing loud music. I had no idea at the time what the hell they were up to. Then that giant moving van shows up with the big green Mayflower boat painted on the side of it. You remember that?"

"No, I don't remember that. Where was I?"

"I have no earthly idea. Maybe in school. Probably that."

"Probably so."

"Well, anyhow, your mother has the whole kit and kaboodle shipped out there COD to Arizona where he was shacked up with that new girl of his."

"Who, Dad?"

"Yes. 'Dad'! Your father. Somewhere in Arizona. I forget." The old man starts cackling and hacking at the same time. He flicks his Pall Mall but the ash misses and floats whole to the floor. "I'd have given fifty bucks to see his face the day that moving van showed up at his door! And here he thought he'd got off scot-free with that new woman of his."

"I must've been in school. I don't remember any of this."

"Gigantic Mayflower moving van; took up the whole damn street just about. And your mother down there shoveling away with a vengeance. Hours she was down there. Her and that 'Kitty,' piling stuff up; throwing things around. I never saw her work so hard. And singing! The two of them. Singing away like it was Mardi Gras or something. All the junk he'd collected his whole life probably. Old photographs of cattle, train magazines, busted guitars, quarter horse trophies; all of it totally ruined and warped outta shape. I kept looking down from the kitchen window. I could see the whole fandango from up there. They didn't know I was watching them. Those movers kept loading box after box of that junk onto the van. They couldn't believe she wanted to actually ship that crap halfway across America. I remember them loading that old buffalo rug of his. Must've weighed as much as the bull it came off of; all dripping with rainwater and smelling like the Wild West." The old man laughs and stretches his newly trimmed toes. He looks down at them, examining the evenness of the cuts. "Well, at least your mother had a sense of humor. That's one thing we can say about her." The boy stays silent. He turns his head slowly toward the little bay window and stares out at the shining magnolia. He can see bees swarming around the sweet ripe blooms. The grandfather watches him now and has a sudden feeling he's not sure of; a sickening feeling high up in his stomach. It reminds him of the nausea of past losses; past aloneness. Women leaving. Him leaving women. A parade of beauties. All gone. Thank God he was over that. He would like more than anything to protect his grandson from that kind of desolation. He's too young yet to fall in there. He speaks to the boy now with new vigor, trying to make his voice sound like a brand-new day: "Anyhow, what I was thinking was—we could certainly use some help here around the place. You know—dishes, floors, a little dusting maybe. Place hasn't been dusted for months, looks like."

"I dusted a week ago," the boy says as he crosses to the hallway closet and returns with a broom and dustpan and starts sweeping up the nail clippings around the old man's feet.

"You did?"

"Yeah, I dusted all the bookcases and the mantel."

"Well, you shouldn't be doing that. You haven't got time what with your job and everything."

"It's all right."

"I mean, you don't get back home here until supper and by that time you're all played out from loading hay and sacks of feed."

"I don't mind."

"No, you shouldn't be doing that kinda work. Housework. That's not for you. Besides, I kinda miss a woman's touch around the place, don't you?"

"What's a woman's touch?"

"You know—all the little frills. Keeping things neat. The skills of organization. The different smells."

"Smells?"

"Something in the air. I can't explain it. A certain kind of buzz. I find that lacking here lately." The boy shrugs and stands there holding the broom and dustpan out in front of him. The little chunk of fallen ash catches his attention and he watches it roll gently back and forth between the old man's leathery feet. He can't believe he's missed it. He flicks it into the dustpan with the corner of the broom. "Do you miss your mother?" the old man asks him flatly. The boy is surprised by the electric jolt through the top of his head that the question triggers. The way the whole world stops around him.

"No," he says.

"You never think about her?"

"No."

"Well, in any case, I think it's not a bad idea to ask that young girl if she'd like to earn some extra cash. She could be real helpful around here, a girl like that."

"What girl?" the boy asks in a trance, picturing his mother's red hair.

"The waitress girl! The one we've been talking about."

"I can't ask her something like that."

"*I'll* ask her then. We'll go down there tonight and I'll ask her."

"Tonight?"

"Yes. Why not? We'll go to supper down at the Inn. Just like before. I'll order the crispy duck and you can have your tuna melt. We'll ask her then. What time do you get off today?"

"Same as usual."

"Good. Come straight home. We'll shower and dress up. Then we'll walk to supper down by the river. I like the walk."

"All right," the boy says halfheartedly.

"Don't forget now. Don't dawdle."

The river cuts through the heart of town. As the boy walks to his job down at the feed store he watches the water moving slowly in wide green sheets. He thinks of Mina. He knows her name quite well. He says her name to himself and smiles. The sound of it makes him laugh. The sound of her name pushes him into a little trot and he kicks out at a squashed beer can, sending it spinning down the rocky bank. He can't believe how just the thought of her transforms his breath. He starts running down Mission, past the saddle shop, past the pit bull that always charges him, then retreats screaming like a coward when he stops short and turns on it. He laughs at his power over dogs and runs on. He can feel Mina's long waist, her ribs under the light cotton dress; the way her back always breaks out in hot bands of sweat when he touches her breasts. He can taste her neck and feel the deep tremble in her chest as she pulls him tight to her and wraps her leg high up around him whispering Spanish in his ear.

FOREIGNERS

Ceiling's this faint bluish like the sky. Got this certain kinda glint about it. Flies won't settle on it, that's for sure. I've watched 'em. Never seen one dare. They're allergic—that's what it is. Must be. Something in the paint. Sidewalls is stock white with a teeny bit a peach throwed in. Just a drip. Gives a glow in midday. Truly. Subtle like. Seats is all green like youse settin' in a cool area with bushes all around. Floor's deep brown—as much like dirt as possible—outdoors. Make it look as much like a picnic as you possibly can. Stimulates the appetite. People seem to enjoy that. Sell a lotta cobbler that way. A whole lotta cobbler. Sells trinkets too. Silver and whatnots. Turquoise and knickknacks. Them little sombrero ashtray dealies. Sold a lotta them. Time was, me and the wife'd take that yellow Coupe DeVille out to Gallop and back. Think nothin' of it, trip like that. Jest pick us up and go. Back when pawn was cheap. Load up on that Indian stuff, then drag it back here to the cafe and sell it. No law against it. Sell it right here at the counter alongside the glazed doughnuts and the chewing gum. Folks'd pause there at the cash register waitin' to pay their bill and their eye'd get caught on all that Indian stuff. Specially easterners. They never seen anything like it. Silver concho belts and feathered war bonnets and whatnot. You could get that stuff cheap back then. They'd walk outta here with an armload a stuff cost ten times what their meal did. They was happy about it too. We towed us a four-horse slat-sided trailer along behind that Coupe DeVille back then and lemme tell ya we loaded her right to the gills. Put over 400,000 miles on that Coupe back and forth to Gallop. Me and the wife. Course we went other places too. Side trips. Went clear on out to Ludlow, California, once for "Mule Days." That was somethin'. Camped right out under the stars too. Never seen so many. Desert seems to bring 'em out more. Went up to Santa Fe once too but that was a different deal. I'll tell ya somethin'—I was born and raised right down there close to Las Cruces, near the Staked Plains country, but when me and the wife went on up there to Santa Fe that was the first time in my life I ever felt like a foreigner. And I'll grant you I never been to Europe or across the pond at all but that was the very first time I ever felt like I didn't belong someplace. Didn't like that feeling one little bit. Me and the wife were sure glad to get back here to the cafe after that. Truth is I'd rather stay home anymore. Just ain't worth venturing out. No bargains left to speak of. Somebody's already put a price on it, seems like.

LIVING THE SIGN

There's a little handmade cardboard sign hanging over the steaming chicken wings that reads: "LIFE IS WHAT'S HAPPENING TO YOU WHILE YOU'RE MAKING PLANS FOR SOMETHING ELSE." The splattered sign twirls slowly under the rays of the orange warming lamps. Apocalypse background music moans from hidden speakers. There's a skinny, anemic-looking kid lurking behind the counter with his cap pulled down tight and his fuzzy pink ears sticking out. Each ear is carrying more rings than a curtain rod and it looks like they've been inserted with a device for tagging cattle. His black cap says "WINGS" on the front; "WINGS" in white. The skinny kid is coping with the computer keyboard and the phone at the same time, pummeling those little clacking brown buttons and squishing the phone with his neck. Another phone right beside him rings for a takeout order and a young girl wearing the same kind of cap, ponytail flouncing out the back, leaps across the skinny kid, knocking the phone to the floor. "Shit!" she says, and scrambles for it; picks it up backwards and mashes it to her ear. It's making a humming, disconnected sound. She slams it down. "Can I help you?" she says to me.

"Yes, I'd like the single order of ten wings, please."

"What kinda sauce?"

"What do you have?" She gives me an exasperated look like she's way too busy to be dealing with anyone who doesn't know the procedure.

"It's all right up there on the board in the little yellow square," she says. "Regular. Medium Hot, and Hot Hot."

"Hot Hot?" I say.

"That's right. Double Hot."

"I'll take the Medium Hot."

"Good," she says, then scribbles the order and slaps it across to two more skinny guys in black caps and long black aprons tending the deep-fry baskets.

"Who wrote the sign?" I ask the girl.

"Excuse me?"

"Who wrote that sign right there, hanging over the chicken?"

"I have no idea," she says, even more peeved that I'm demanding her attention beyond the call of duty.

"I'd like to meet him."

"Who?" she says in disbelief.

"Whoever wrote the sign."

"I don't *know* who wrote the sign," she whines.

"Does anybody here know?" Now she swings her mighty hips toward the two skinny fry-cooks, whipping her ponytail past my nose.

"Anybody know who wrote this sign? Guy here wants to know."

"What?" the fry-cooks say, almost in unison, as they jiggle my wings in the sputtering oil and shake giant silver salt and pepper shakers over the whole mess.

"Who wrote the sign hanging here? This guy wants to know."

"Not me," says one of them, dumping my greasy wings in a

white paper basket while the other guy pours a red gelatinous goo all over them. The girl whips back around to face me.

"What to drink?" she says.

"Coke," I say. "Small Coke."

"Pepsi all right?"

"That's all you've got?"

"That's all we've got."

"I'll take it," I say, and she pops an empty cup down on the counter in front of me, then slides the basket of red wings over.

"That'll be three forty-seven," she says.

"So, nobody knows who wrote the sign?" I persist as I probe for my wallet.

"That's right. Nobody seems to know."

"Maybe it was somebody on a different shift?"

"That's possible."

"I'd like to talk to that person if I could," I tell her as I hand her a ratty-looking ten.

"Why is that?"

"I'd like to see if the person who wrote that sign is actually living it or if he's just talking through his hat."

"Living what?" she says.

"The sign. The meaning of the sign."

"Look, I don't know *who* wrote the sign, okay?" she says as she deals my change back to me with finality.

"Well, have you noticed any one of the employees on the other shifts being particularly auspicious? Particularly present and attentive? Almost buoyant, maybe?"

"I'm not on the other shifts. I'm on this one," she says.

"That's true, but maybe you've heard about this person. He's probably notorious by now. Fun to be around."

"*What* person?"

"The one who wrote the sign."

"Look, sir, I don't know who wrote the sign. *Somebody* wrote the sign but it wasn't me. Okay?"

"*I* wrote the sign," the kid with the pulled-down cap and the ears sticking out says as he hangs the phone up softly and rubs the back of his neck.

"*You* wrote the sign?" The girl giggles and turns to the other two. "Dicky wrote the sign!"

"What sign?" the fry-cooks say in total unison.

"This sign! This sign right here!" She bats the sign with the back of her hand, causing it to spin wildly above the steaming wings.

"What's it say?" one of the cooks asks halfheartedly.

"You can read," she says, and the skinniest fry-cook slouches over to the sign, rubbing his wet red fingers on the black apron. He reaches up and stops the sign from dancing. He squints and reads it.

"I don't get it," he says, backing up a step and sucking some of the sauce off his thumb.

"It says: 'LIFE IS WHAT'S HAPPENING TO YOU WHILE YOU'RE MAKING PLANS FOR SOMETHING ELSE,'" the girl informs him.

"I know what it *says*. I can read."

"Well?" she says.

"Dicky wrote that?"

"What's it mean, Dicky?" the girl asks seductively, making a wispy mysterious voice.

"Just what it says," Dicky mumbles.

"It's very sharp," I say. "Where'd you get that?"

"Just made it up," Dicky says.

"Just out of the blue?" I ask him. I still haven't seen his face. He keeps diddling with the computer keys, sniffling slightly under the long bill of his cap.

"Yeah, it just like came to me."

"Dicky's a smart dude," the fry-cook says as he jabs Dicky in the ribs with his elbow and heads back to his post. Dicky jumps slightly but doesn't reveal his face. I talk to the top of his cap.

"So, Dicky, did this thought occur to you in a moment when you saw yourself consumed by dreams of the future and realized life was passing you by?"

"Something like that," he mumbles.

"Did it arrive as a kind of shock; a jolt of awareness where you suddenly saw how far away from reality you actually were?"

"Did what arrive?"

"The thought. The smart thought that life was what was happening to you while you were making plans for something else?" He sniffles again and wipes his nose with the back of his wrist. Now he looks up at me; deep grayish green eyes with dark purple half-moons under them, like he's been in a recent bad wreck. More rings; one hanging from each nostril and a set of three silver ones in his lower lip that look like they might be starting to fester. His eyes are soft and frightened, darting away from me toward the plate-glass window.

"I wasn't planning anything really," he says, almost in a whisper as though protecting himself from being overheard by the others. "I mean I was like dreaming about Colorado."

"Colorado?"

"Yeah." His eyes flash past me again, catching mine for a scared millisecond, then scrambling across the computer keys hunting for a place to hide.

"Daydreaming, you mean?"

"Yeah. I was right here. Just like this. I was staring out that window." The ponytail girl has now retreated back behind the gurgling sinks of hot oil with the two fry-cooks. She's engaging them in conspiratorial tones, lighting a cigarette and taking paranoid peeks at me over her shoulder. Dicky's green eyes leap back to the plate-glass window and fix on the dripping beads of condensation. Outside on the street, it looks cold. It is cold.

"How long ago was this, Dicky?"

"What?" he says in a trance.

"That you were having this daydream about Colorado?"

"I don't know. Like just the other day, I guess. I was just standing here. I was watching the snow."

"Snow? It was snowing then?"

"No. Like in Colorado. I was watching it snow in Colorado."

"But you were here?"

"Yeah, I was right here. Just like this. I could see it coming down. Like very soft. Everything was quiet. Like real peaceful. There was this cabin on the mountain behind me."

"You saw yourself out there in the snow? In Colorado?"

"Yeah. I was there. I mean I was here but I was out there. And I don't know how I got out there exactly. Like I kinda wished myself out there, I guess. I'd been thinking about it for a long time."

"Colorado?"

"Yeah. I was right there. And like I kept seeing this cabin through the falling snow. Like golden light in the windows and smoke coming out the chimney. You know—and like firewood stacked up on the porch. But something was missing."

"What was that?"

"This girl."

"Oh. Your girlfriend?"

"No, this girl I'd like imagined would be out there."

"She wasn't there?"

"No. And that kinda like shocked me, you know?"

"Who was this girl?"

60

"I don't know, but she wasn't anywhere around."

"An imaginary girl?"

"I guess. Yeah, I guess so. She wasn't out there."

"So you were disappointed about that?"

"Yeah, I was. Like that was the whole reason I'd come out of the cabin in the first place."

"Oh, you'd been *inside* the cabin?"

"Yeah, but she wasn't in there so I came outside in the snow and I was like looking back at it, seeing the lights and the smoke, but she wasn't anywhere around. You know, like I was totally alone out there. And then I thought like why'd I come all the way out here to be totally alone? I had this like awful feeling about it. You know that feeling like you're going to be sick. Like you might not ever see a human being again. Just—like alone. That's all."

"Is that when you had the thought?"

"What thought?"

"The thought that life is what's happening to you while you're making plans for something else?"

"I guess," he says, and his eyes come back to me for a beat, then flee to the window again. "I don't know. No, I didn't have the thought right then. The thought came like later, I think."

"Later?"

"Yeah, later."

"After what?"

"I don't know. After like something snapped; something popped right behind me. I think it was the oil."

"Oh, for the wings? The fry oil?"

"Yeah. It started popping and crackling like—you know, when you throw fresh wings in there it kinda like explodes."

"Right. So that brought you back here, when you heard that?"

"Yeah. I came back here."

61

"And Colorado went away?"

"Yeah. It just like disappeared."

"And that's when you had the thought?"

"It must've been," he says, and vanishes under the brim of his cap again.

"I'm proud of you, Dicky," I tell him, and reach out and pat him on his cap, right above the word "WINGS."

I grab my empty cup and basket of wings and head for the Pepsi dispenser. There's one group of Asian college students sitting in a long booth. Two pretty girls and a boy with thick glasses. The girls are giggling and spitting their soft drinks while the boy sucks on his wings. I take the booth right behind them. The place is otherwise empty of customers. Two mute TVs are mounted high in separate corners. One, tuned to NFL replays and the other is some Discovery Channel showing a snake slowly devouring a huge yellow egg. As soon as I'm seated I see Dicky heading over in my direction, head down, shuffling toward me with his hands in his pockets. He slides into the booth and sits right across from me, keeping his face hidden behind his cap.

"It's not exactly true," he whispers right off.

"What?"

"About the sign. I mean like *I* wrote the sign and everything; I hung it up there but it wasn't my idea. I mean like, what the sign says—that was another dude's idea. It wasn't mine."

"Oh," I say.

"He's the dude you wanna meet. You know how you were saying he might be different and stuff?"

"Oh, yeah."

"Well, he's the dude you wanna meet."

"Who is he?"

"Bruce. Bruce is the dude who thought it up."

"Who's Bruce?"

"He's the dude who does all my piercing. He put all these rings in."

"Oh," I say.

"He's totally awesome. You should meet Bruce. He's got all kinds of ideas like that."

"Where is Bruce?"

"He's around. I could like track him down if you want."

"Well, I'm kind of just passing through, Dicky."

"Oh," he says, and starts to hoist himself up out of the booth, keeping both hands in his pockets. "I just thought maybe you wanted to meet him. You said you wanted to meet the person who like wrote the sign."

"I met you." He hangs there at the corner of the booth, teetering between going and staying.

"But I'm not the one, see. I mean like he told me that thing—Bruce did—what the sign says. He told me that like a long time ago and I remembered it 'cause I thought it was like cool, you know. So I just wrote it down, but I wasn't the one who thought it up."

"I know that."

"It wasn't me."

"But you wrote it down. You cut that little piece of cardboard very carefully and found a Magic Marker and wrote all the words down in capital letters. Then you covered the whole thing with strips of invisible tape so the words wouldn't get splattered with chicken grease and you punched that little hole in the top and threaded that shoelace through it and then you climbed up there, above the wings, balancing and maneuvering your fingers through the electric wires, tying the knot so that it would hang dead center just below the lamps in plain sight of anyone who might come in, right at eye level where you knew the eye would be seduced into reading it and the mind would then turn it over, replacing for just a second any thought about food or hunger with a new thought that might turn them toward the actual plain fact of living and away from dreaming about the stock market or their girlfriend or their failed marriage or their history grades or even Armageddon. And in that flashing moment some mysterious light explodes through their whole body, sending signals to a remote part of themselves that suddenly remembers being born and just as certainly knows it's bound to die. You did that, Dicky. That's what you did."

"Yeah, I guess," he mumbles, and shuffles back to work, giving me a little good-bye wave with his pale fingers flicking. The soft clacking of computer keys starts up again. The snake has completely devoured the egg; the huge bulge of it inching midway down its body. The Asian students are cleaning up their booth; wiping red sauce off the Formica tabletop. Brett Favre throws a bullet into the end zone. A frantic female vocalist enters the background music with no pretense of developing a melody line. I stare down at my basket of wings. They seem far away. I have no idea what town I'm in. It doesn't matter. I have no idea what town I'm going to. I have no plans.

THE COMPANY'S INTEREST

I mean, he tells me: "Three drive-offs and you're history." Noling.
That's what he says to me first day of work. Three. What am I supposed to do? I'm one lone woman out here. I'm two miles off the
Interstate and a good ten to town. What does he expect? I see a car
pull up. Four in the morning. Car looks cool to me. Indiana plates.
Kinda clean. White guy and his family. Looks like his family anyhow. Woman and two babies. How am I supposed to know? Maybe
he's kidnapped the whole bunch. I go ahead and authorize the car
on the speaker. I'm all alone. I'm trying to make my voice sound
big. Like a guy or something. Deep. You know, like there's more
than just one of me. Like I'm backed up by a whole bad-ass gang of
truckers in here. I'm watching from the cash counter. I can see the
guy plain as day. He keeps staring straight at the pump, watching
the numbers roll over. He never once looks back at me. Not once.
No reason to be suspicious, right? His wife's jiggling one of the kids
on her knee; fooling with some stupid feather or something; tick-
ling the kid in the face. Baby's giggling. I can see that. I've got a
clear view from here. I can see every pump on the place. He's the
only car out there. Guy even washes his damn windshield. Does a
real careful job too; cleaning off the squeegee with a paper towel
between strokes; making sure there's no drip marks. Real careful

like. Still never looks back at me. Not once. Now, you know, a drive-off's usually gonna give you some hint, some clue somewhere. A drive-off never cleans his damn windshield. He's too busy thinking about escape. Too worried the whole time. Not this guy. He takes his sweet time. This guy finishes the windshield; wipes his head-lights; goes around to the back; cleans off the taillights; dips the squeegee again; washes the rear window; dumps the squeegee back in the tub; climbs in the damn car and drives off. Just drives right the fuck off into the night. Never skipped a beat. Now, what am I sup-posed to do? Go running my fat butt out there, screaming and wav-ing my arms around? Take a chance of getting shot at? How am I supposed to stop him? I'm not armed. I'm one lone woman out here. But Noling, he tells me, two more and I'm toast. That's what he says. Company's gonna take it outta my check. Then, next time, when I *do* ask a car for a prepay, credit card, cash security, or some-thing, he tells me that's not legal. State law or some shit. I can't do that. What am I supposed to do? He says, Just don't let it happen again. It's my responsibility to watch out for the company's inter-est. I mean like the other night for instance; these two come rolling in here real late with Kentucky plates. And they were some sorry-lookin' road meat, let me tell you. Beat-to-stew truck, all rusted out, fenders flapping, cow flop dripping off the mud flaps, gun rack; the whole nine yards. Flat scary. And these two come sloshing outta this truck and I'm tellin' you, between the both of them they had to have tipped close to nine hundred, no lie. I mean I'm good at weights. I can eyeball weights within five pounds from watchin' Daddy sort feeder calves. I'm real good at it. And these guys had to total every bit of nine hundred, believe you me. And here they come; raggedy beards, hair down to their asses, tattoos. No socks either. I could see that clear from here. That's how good my eyes are. Real deep-woods animals, these two. Suspicion wrote all over 'em. Whole time they're pumping gas their eyes are jumping all around. They stare at me; they stare at the road; they stare back at me. I was praying they *would* drive off so I wouldn't have to face them. I mean, can you imagine? One lone woman, middle of nowhere, and these two come cruising in? One thing I do is scribble down their plate number so at least I'll have that to show Noling when he gets all ashy with me next day. But I look up and they're *not* driving off; they're coming in! They're heading right for the doors, straight toward me, the both of them. And now my heart is really going to town because if these two were scary at a distance, now they're like a horror show. Big beefy arms swinging; spittin' huge gobs of black shit and neither one of 'em's talking. That's what got me going. No talk. Not one peep out of either one of 'em the whole time. And I'm all alone, understand. Not a soul in the store. I mean I can usually handle it all right if I hear some talk between 'em or a chuckle or something but these two were stone silent. I just can't stand that. I mean I've always got something on like the radio or TV or something so it breaks the air up; gets the loneliness out. Makes me feel like company. But silence drives me right up the tree. And so now, in they come and I'm thinking, "Oh shit, this is it," but instead of coming toward me they head right for the candy aisle, real slow, swinging those big meaty arms of theirs. They're so fat their arms hang straight out with daylight under-neath 'em. Like the way you see a tom turkey get puffed up; that's the way they're moving. Real slow, up and down the candy aisle and the only sound is their key chains clinking on their hips. They have matching key chains all jammed up with them miniature wrenches and jackknives; church keys and these big black iron crosses like bikers wear. You know, them German jobs like Harley shit. All matching. And here they are cruising the candy, big as life. Both of 'em. Like a couple a dumb-ass bears lost out on the highway. They never once look over at me. They just stare at the candy. They pick up the M&M's and look at the label, then toss the bags up and down like they're checking the weight or something. I can't figure it out. I mean when was the last time you checked out the contents on a bag of M&M's? Both of 'em keep doing this. Not a word between 'em. They go to the PayDays and do the same thing: tossing them; checking the labels; smelling the wrappers. Then they go to the Tootsie Rolls; the Almond Joys; the Reese's peanut butter cups. Up and down the aisle; back and forth. By the time they reach the end they've got their sausage arms loaded with candy bars. Both of 'em with exactly the same candy. I can see that from the cash counter. I'm watching real careful out the sides of my eyes, trying to keep track of what they've got; watching out for the company's interest. And all the time I'm thinking they're gonna rob the joint for sure. This candy thing is just a stall while they check the place out; the TV surveillance; the exits; alarms and shit. Any second now they're gonna wig out and pull some monster gun on me. That's what I'm thinking. But no. Now they go to the potato chip aisle and start piling on bags of Fritos, Cool Ranch chips, Ruffles, pretzels. I mean you can't believe the stuff. And each of 'em keeps picking up the exact same thing as the other one; like they're afraid one of 'em's gonna get something the other one doesn't have. Couple a big bearded babies. Then they turn around toward me. At the end of the aisle they stop and turn straight toward me and I'm thinking this is really it. Now I've really had it. They've got their goodies piled high as their noses. Just their little squinty black eyes peeping out over the top. And suddenly I see that they're twins! Just by the eyes. You know how you can recognize something like that. Just by seeing something in the eyes. You just know they're related. And now my heart is thumping so bad I'm afraid they're gonna see my name tag jumping right off my tit! I'm just sure they're gonna pull a gun on me now. They're gonna walk right up to the counter; dump their piles of junk; pull a big .357 magnum and stick it right in my round mouth. I'm sure I'm gonna die. There's no way out of it. I'm all alone here. What am I supposed to do? Call 911? Time the highway patrol gets out here I'll be dead. And I'm shaking all over now. My armpits are dripping. My fingers have all gone cold and I start thinking about Mama. Out of the blue I'm thinking about her. I start to see her sitting on the sofa, watching *Oprah;* smoking reds; eating Cheeze Whiz and Ritz crackers; crying big tears over all the bad-luck people on the show. I don't know what's gonna happen; who's gonna take care of her when I'm gone; who's gonna tell her I've just got my brains blown out down at the Conoco. There's nobody. I'm the only one left. I don't know how it ever got like this.

CONCEPCIÓN

My dad consulted gypsies on a regular basis. It was something we never talked about—me and my mother—but it was true. Reason I know is, one night he pulled over suddenly in front of a little stone house on the back side of a lemon grove out past Upland. My mom and I were in the car—me dressed in my choir robes from church and her in a navy blue suit with a little pillbox hat and purse to match. It was around Easter time and there'd been some big service with the men's and boys' choirs combined. My mom was very proud of my voice, she said, although I don't see how she could have possibly picked it out from all those dozens of other voices. How she could have heard just mine. She sat in the passenger seat right in front of me and we both watched out the windows as my dad stood on the porch of the stone house under a yellow light ringing the doorbell. He was all decked out in his Air Force uniform with tiny moths and mosquito hawks cutting circles just above his captain's hat. He was staring out past the lemon trees and the far-away lights of San Dimas as he waited for an answer at the door and never once looked back to us in the car. He seemed to have a lot on his mind, but whatever it was we weren't included. The heavy sweet smell of lemon blossoms came right through the glass. There was a sign propped in the window of the little stone house that read

"CONCEPCIÓN"—just that one word, handwritten in orange crayon with little blue Christmas lights around the border. A small porcelain crucifix hung right above the sign and the bright blood from Christ's wounds seemed to stand out even more intensely against the pure enameled white of his skin. Finally someone came to the door and let my dad in. I couldn't make out the face but I knew it was a woman by the way she softly shut the door and I saw the red ruffle of her long skirt disappear behind my father's khakis. My mom and I sat in silence for a long while, listening to coyotes and the high shriek of owls diving for field mice in the orchard. The Santa Ana winds were blowing in from the east. My mother shifted the purse around on her lap and stared out the windshield. I had no idea what she was thinking.

"What's that word mean?" I asked her.

"What word, sweetie?"

"That orange word in the window."

"Oh, that's Spanish or something," she said after turning her head to read it.

"Spanish for what?"

"I have no idea, honey. I never took Spanish." We fell silent again and I kept staring at the light behind the green curtains of the stone house but I couldn't see any silhouettes. My mother popped open her purse and took out some Kleenex. She started patting her lips with it very slowly and making a quiet smacking sound. She took out a little round mirror and examined the corners of her mouth. I don't know what she was looking for. She had a perfect mouth.

"What's Dad doing in there?" I said.

"Just—paying a visit," she said, still looking at her face in the mirror.

"Who is it? Who is it he's visiting?"

"Just a friend of his, I guess."

"You don't know her?"

"No, I've never met her, sweetie."

"Can we go in and meet her?"

"No, honey, that wouldn't be a good idea."

"Why not?"

"Well—your father has private things to say to her."

"What kind of things?"

"Well—you know—things like—" she paused and looked out the windshield as an owl flashed past. She dropped the little mirror back into her purse and looked down at it as though she'd just remembered something that had to do with a shopping list.

"Things like what?" I asked again.

"Things like— Well—we both go to church—you and I. Grandma goes to church. Most of our family—"

"Church?"

"Yes. We all go to church. Most people go to church. Most people believe in— Well—your father doesn't."

"What?"

"Go to church. He doesn't believe in church."

"How come?"

"I'm not really sure, sweetheart. I've never asked him. It's none of my business really. But he has questions—certain questions, just like we all do."

"What questions?"

"Well—things like—mysterious things. You know. Things we can't answer on our own." She stuffed the Kleenex back in her bag and snapped it shut. The snapping seemed to close the issue and she went back into her silent stare out the front window. The choir gown was stifling and I started pulling it off, over my head, but it got stuck around my neck. A quick panic flashed through me like

I'd suddenly fallen into a pit. It was pitch black inside and smelled like starch. A yelp came out of me like I'd heard dogs make when you surprise them in their sleep. "You have to unsnap the back of the collar first, sweetheart. You can't just yank it off. Here, let me help you with it." I felt my mother's thin fingers fishing for the metal hooks that fastened the starched white collar to the heavy black cloth at the back of my neck. Her fingers felt far away. The panic grew and seemed to swarm toward my eyes. I saw the red ruffled skirt go flying past me in the darkness. Its rustle blew right across my head like the wind outside. I couldn't tell which was which. "Now don't twitch around," my mother said. "I'm trying to find these darn hooks. Just sit still!" But I couldn't. The fear became like a trapped miner's when the shaft collapses. There was no light at all. A white dog with red eyes appeared, running straight at me. I jerked up hard on the thick black fabric and heard all the stitching pop out. My head came free. "Now you've gone and torn it! Look at that! You've ripped the collar right out. Oh brother. What're we going to do?" My mother gathered up the ripped gown and turned back around in her seat with it, examining the collar.

"Sorry," I said, lamely. I was so glad to be breathing sweet air again.

"You can't just rip these things off like a T-shirt or something, honey. These are specially made. They have professional seamstresses do this work."

"Sorry," I said again.

"This doesn't belong to us, you know. It's church property. Now I'm going to have to see if I can restitch the whole thing."

I sat back in the seat and looked out the window toward the stone house as my mother put on her glasses and began picking thread out of the torn collar with her red enameled nails. She switched on the dome light in the Plymouth and, just as she did that, I saw the tall thin shape of my father pass behind the green curtains. Then the woman's form followed him. The door opened and I saw my father hand the woman some money, then put his Air Force captain's hat on and head back toward the car. As he came down the narrow path through the yard I saw him put a small brown bag into his pocket. My mother quickly rolled up the torn choir robe and stuffed it in the back seat beside me.

"Now, don't you say one word about this to your father. You promise?"

"I won't," I said.

"Not one word," she said as she smoothed her skirt down and placed her purse back in her lap as though she hadn't moved an inch the whole time he'd been gone.

No one spoke on the way back. It wasn't far, maybe five miles back to the house, but no one spoke a word. I kept looking down at the black choir gown, trying to see if it was possible for anyone to tell if it was ripped. It looked collapsed and defeated like it was never going to live up to its expectations. Some kind of fallen angel maybe.

When we got home my dad walked straight off into the avocado orchard without saying anything. My mom and I went into the house. We turned the kitchen light on and sat down at the Formica table across from each other. She'd brought the choir robe with her and took her glasses out again to examine the collar.

"What's Dad doing out there?" I said.

"Sweetie, I don't know what he's doing. I don't ask. It's none of my business," she said, and she never looked up at me at all, just kept fiddling with that stiff collar. I stood up and went to the door. "Where are you going, honey?"

"Just outside," I said.

"Well, don't bother your father. He needs to be alone right now."

"I won't," I said.

Outside, the wind was still blowing down from the foothills. It was a warm fast wind that shook through the avocado trees and left big columns of dust clear down to the road, then stopped dead still. The dust settled through the silver yard light on the machine shed and I thought I caught a glimpse of my dad disappearing behind the corrugated-metal wall where the tractor was parked. I circled around behind the shed on the other side and my breath started to pick up for fear he'd catch me spying on him. I waited for the next blast of wind to cover my movements and I went quick, trying to Scotch-hop through the broad dry leaves on the ground. When I got up behind the old acacia tree I saw my dad kneeling behind the shed, facing the metal wall. He was very close to the wall and had his back to the orchard. He took off his captain's hat and laid it on the ground beside him. I could see the silver flight wings gleaming in the light. He took the little brown bag out of his pocket and pulled out a small yellow candle. He lit the candle with his Zippo and set it on a smooth stone at the base of the wall. The wind came up again but the flame hardly bent at all. My dad stared down at it for the longest time with his hands resting on his thighs. He just stared straight into the flickering light as the wind hummed through the rafters of the shed roof and the reflection of the flame bounced off the corrugated wall. He closed his eyes and bowed his head. Then, finally, he brought his hands together and squeezed them tight. His lips never moved, though. I watched them very closely but they never moved at all.

IT WASN'T PROUST

Far in the Great North Woods there's a deep black lake; one of tens of thousands in that lonely region. This one's a man-made lake in a perfect diamond shape. It freezes so thick in the winter you can drive a one-ton truck right out into the middle of it and ice fish for pike and giant muskie. In the summer it's alive with beaver, blue heron, green frogs, wood duck, and a pair of red-eyed loons that warble in that eerie tone reminiscent of the timber wolf. Deer and bearded moose sometimes emerge like magic from the dark woods and water out of the south bank, then slip back into the thick tamarack and pines. On the opposite shore a little portable aluminum dock on rubber wheels juts out into the iron-stained water. It has two orange lawn chairs chained to the end of it so they don't blow away in the late afternoon thunderstorms that sweep in off the southern plains regular as clockwork. Every morning at the height of the summer season, a married couple meet on this dock with their white cups of coffee; cups that say "Betty's Pies" in blue with a little steaming pie etched right below the logo. They unchain the lawn chairs and adjust them, facing due west with the rising sun just over their left shoulders. They sit within arm's reach of each other so their fingers can brush and make little twitching signs of recognition and affection. They've been coming up here for eighteen years; sitting on this very same dock in these very same chairs. Sometimes they just stare at the glistening flat surface of the water and the slow-motion clouds, pink-edged from the sun like cotton candy. Other times they talk:

What exactly is this thing you have about the French?

What thing?

This derision all the time; this attitude. Now the kids have picked it up.

They have?

Yes, they have. I don't want them growing up with an attitude like that. I want them to travel; go places; be open-minded.

To France? You want them to travel to France?

Yes. Of course. I'd really like them to see France. Why not?

Well, they can see France if they want to. I don't care if they see France.

They're not going to want to see France if they already have this thing about it.

What thing?

They make fun of the accent. They think everything French is pretentious and stupid.

Well, they're right about that.

It's not funny, Henry. You might think it's funny but they don't understand that kind of sarcasm. They're too young. They think it's serious.

It *is* serious.

I can't talk to you.

A long pause now in which nothing happens but the continuous rippling motion of the inky water so that they both have the sensation they're sitting on the bow of a giant ship getting nowhere. The loon just drifts out there in the middle, looking like a wooden decoy, then suddenly dives for fish, leaving shimmering silver rings expanding across the dark water. They both keep their eyes on these rings, waiting for the loon to reemerge; counting the seconds in silence; "one thousand one; one thousand two; one thousand three . . ." They've done this many times before over the years and neither of them can remember how the ritual first got started.

Shall I tell you a story?

Sure, why not. What kind of story is it going to be?

The story of how I first came by this derisive attitude toward the French.

Oh boy.

(The loon pops up but they've both lost track of the seconds.)

I was in Paris. This was years ago, in the sixties, wandering around with some girl.

What girl was this now?

It doesn't matter.

Was this the girl you'd met on crystal methedrene in a teepee in Woodstock?

No. It was just some girl I'd run into. I can't remember.

You remember. You remember all your girls.

Can I just tell you this?

Sure. I'm all ears.

I'd gone out late one night for a walk.

Without the girl?

That's right. She stayed. She wanted to read or something.

Proust, I'll bet.

What?

Remembrance of Things Past?

Oh, never mind. I thought you might like to hear this.

I *do* want to hear this. I'm just trying to fill in the picture. You went out walking the streets of Paris in the middle of the night and left your girl behind reading Proust. Then what?

All right. Now, this was back in the days when I was still drinking. And I was just wandering around the streets. I did a lot of wandering in those days.

What were you looking for?

Nothing. I'd just wander. I liked to wander.

You were looking for women.

I *had* a woman.

You were looking for more women. You weren't satisfied with just one. You wanted more.

Could I just go on with this please and not get sidetracked by every little—

Sure. Go on with it. I'm just trying to keep tabs.

(Another pause while they watch a painted turtle stick its neck up through the lily pads and blow water out its slitted nostrils.)

I had these romantic notions in my head back then about Paris being some kind of last bastion of true writers. You know, full of old haunts where you might brush up against the ghosts of Blaise Cendrars or Vallejo or Céline or Villon. You know—so I was kind of looking for these old hangouts I'd heard about; bars and—but I had no idea where they might be or what their names were, so I just kept stumbling into places that looked kind of old and seedy and ordering Pernod and sitting around watching people and listening, but since I couldn't understand a word of French I had no clue what was going on and no way to ask anyone.

First step—learn the language. Always learn the language.

Right. It's not my language. I have no affinity with it. The sound— all that guttural stuff. The spitting.

Spitting? There's no spitting in French. It's very precise.

Anyway, I kept this up all night, going from one bar to the next, drinking along the way, until I finally found a place where there were some people speaking English. The bartender spoke English and there were some girls—

Ah, more girls! You found them.

They were Scandinavian types but they were speaking perfect English, so I started talking to them.

Why not.

Anyhow, I was already half in the bag from drinking at all the bars along the way when one of these Scandinavian women comes up and sits down right beside me. Right off the bat like that. Then I thought, well, this must be the normal deal in Paris: women just coming right up and acting friendly like that. So, first thing she does is order a bottle of wine and two glasses. Real cheap wine, I could tell from the label, and she pours me a drink. I say no thanks because I'm drinking bourbon and Pernod and—actually I'd lost track but I knew wine would really mess me up at that point so I refused. But she insists and she's got these sad eyes so—

Oh brother.

What?

"Sad eyes"?

Yeah. That's right. Something very weary and touching about them even though she's very young. So, anyhow, I sip a little wine with her and get to talking. Turns out she's an ex-model, kind of over-the-hill; pushing thirty or something. That's old for a model, I guess.

I thought she was very young? You said she had sad eyes but she was very young.

I thought she was very young but I was mistaken. I was pretty loaded.

Apparently.

So, she starts talking and she won't stop. I think she was just waiting for someone to come along so she could unload her whole story. Now listen to this: she says she was discovered one day riding her bicycle down a dusty street in some tiny village in Norway to buy bread for her mother. She's fifteen or sixteen at the time and some sleazeball steps out of a BMW in a slick suit and asks her if she wants to be a high-fashion model. That was it. She goes back and tells her parents the news and her mother's mad because she's forgotten to buy the bread but her father smells money and wants to meet the sleazeball. Next thing they know, the whole family's on a plane to Paris.

The whole family?

Well yeah, she's underage so her parents have to come along to chaperone.

Oh.

So, she comes to Paris and she's an overnight success. She's on the cover of international magazines; she's making big money hand over fist; she travels to New York, Rome, Munich, London; all over the place.

With her parents still?

Still with her parents. I mean, can you imagine—they're all from this little spit of a village in the backwoods of Norway; her dad's a mailman or something, her mother's never been on an airplane in her whole life, and suddenly they're all thrown into this high-powered fashion world with photographers stalking them and agents cutting each other's throats to get a piece of her.

No wonder she looked older than she actually was.

What?

No wonder she had sad eyes.

Right. Anyhow—long story short. After about three or four years of this her father commits suicide.

Oh no!

He throws himself off a cruise ship in the Bahamas and he's never seen again.

My God.

A year later, her mother kills herself.

Stop it.

She does. Hangs herself in a hotel closet. The girl finds her the next morning.

The daughter?

Yeah. Just finds her hanging there with a bathrobe sash tied around her neck.

How old is she now?

The girl?

Yeah. The daughter. The model.

Pushing twenty, I guess.

Twenty. That's still young. So what happens then?

She comes back to Paris and starts using smack.

This is a true story?

That's what she told me.

And you believed her?

Why not?

You'd believe anything with a skirt attached to it.

No, I was way too drunk to care about bagging her. I was just listening.

And this is your provocation for condemning the French? They, somehow, corrupted a poor, innocent little girl from an itty-bitty Norwegian village? That's kind of lame.

No, let me finish.

There's more?

Yeah. She finishes her story and turns away from me and stares into the wine bottle with the most melancholy look. It's almost as though by telling me her tale it's called everything back up for her. I mean the sadness in her eyes is more than I can handle and I start thinking about the girl back at the hotel.

The one reading Proust?

It wasn't Proust!

Just kidding.

I don't know what it was but it wasn't Proust!

Take it easy.

I can't tell you anything without some underlying—

What? Some underlying what?

(They both go silent. A sharp wind creates a rippling line of surf like a miniature tidal wave heading straight toward them. Neither of them acknowledges the unaccountable terror it sparks in them. The man continues his tale but now it's more like he's talking to himself or maybe the reflections of puffy clouds racing across the lake.)

Suddenly I had this overwhelming need to be with her; to be back at the hotel, safe. I don't know what it was. A panic or something. So I pay for my drink—the bourbon I'd ordered—say so long to the Norwegian girl, and head out the door. Well, this bar is kind of underground with a narrow set of stairs leading back up to the street, like a little dungeon kind of. And I'm negotiating these steps as best I can in the condition I'm in, kind of clutching the walls as I climb back up, and I realize I'm in much worse shape than I thought I was and this panic is starting to escalate. I'm starting to hallucinate that I'm in some mini-French hell with the guillotines and the stone walls running with blood and all of a sudden, out of nowhere, come these two bonehead muscleman types up behind me; these two Frog bouncers wearing black turtlenecks and gold chains and they look like they've just stepped out of a Jean-Paul Belmondo movie. They're yelling at me in French, which I don't understand, and one of them barges up in front of me and blocks my way out while the other one behind grabs me by the back of the neck.

What'd they want?

Well, the guy blocking my way figures out I'm American and tells me in broken English—really bad English—that I owe them fifty bucks or something for the bottle of rotgut wine. "What wine?" I say. "I was drinking bourbon." Then all at once it dawns on me through my alcoholic stupor that the Norwegian girl's a hooker and she's just run a scam on me so I get stuck with the overpriced wine.

So, her whole story was just a—fabrication?

Pure make-believe. And I go right through the roof. All my American outrage comes up about being deceived like that by a bunch of sleazy Frogs.

But she was Norwegian.

She was in cahoots with them! And there's no way in hell I'm paying fifty bucks for a bottle of shit wine I never ordered. I didn't have fifty bucks anyhow. So, something in me completely flips out. I break out of this neck hold the guy's got me in and I start spitting and snarling at them, hurling insults, calling them cowards, and I challenge them both to a fistfight up on the street. I mean I could barely stand up, let alone throw a punch. I had to keep one eye closed just to stay focused on them and I'm spitting and drooling all over myself.

Charming. I'm sure the French were impressed.

Yeah, well even through the booze and my one sort of delirious eye I could see that these two guys were absolutely terrified of me.

Insanity's always alarming.

Yeah. I could see it in their eyes. They thought they'd tangled up with a complete wacko. So that only incites me to go further with it. I start screaming and ripping my shirt, smashing the wall with my fist—

Were you having emotional problems back then?

No—I mean no more than normal. I was just outraged by the whole thing.

And ever since then you've carried this grudge against the French?

Pretty much so, yeah.

Just from this one little incident, you condemn an entire culture?

Yeah, I guess so. It wasn't so little at the time.

Wouldn't you say that's extremely narrow-minded of you?

Especially considering you were shit-faced drunk; couldn't speak the language and had no business engaging in conversation with a hooker to begin with?

I had no idea she was a hooker! I took her at face value.

And all the while your innocent young girl is waiting for you back at the hotel, reading Proust and thinking you're out for a little stroll through the streets of Paris.

It wasn't Proust, goddammit! It wasn't Proust!! It had nothing to do with Proust. Why do you have to keep hammering away at that! What the hell is wrong with you anyway! It wasn't goddamn Proust!!

(The man has leaped to his feet in a sudden fury. His outburst is so violent it causes the entire aluminum finger dock to tremble and sway beneath them. He has to grab hold of one of the upright pipes to steady himself. The woman just sits there, staring at the loon again, deeply satisfied that she's caused such an avalanche inside him. On the hill behind them the screen door of the cabin opens and slams with a resounding bang that sends the loon down deep. The couple turn in unison toward the sound to see their nine-year-old son emerge with a bowl of cereal, squinting his eyes against the sun. The woman waves to the boy. The man doesn't. The boy waves back to his mother and drops the bowl of cereal on the stone path. The bowl shatters. Milk splatters. The spoon clatters. The boy runs back inside. After a while, the woman speaks.)

I'd better go up.

No, wait.

(The man sits back down in his orange lawn chair. His knees are weak. His hands are trembling. He feels as though he's done some serious damage to his nervous system. He feels something akin to shame but doesn't want to call it that. He was simply trying to tell a story. He realizes he's been had. The screen door opens and slams again on the hill behind them. They both turn toward the sound and simultaneously have the same impression that they've grown much older. Their necks are stiffer. Their torsos turn in short, jerky increments rather than with the fluid grace they used to know. This impression widens to memories of skinny-dipping in this very same lake when they couldn't keep their hands off each other and their bodies were sleek and shining like the young otters that shared the water with them. The man turns toward the woman and sees her neck; her crossed legs peeking through the yellow bathrobe; her beauty still shining. He reaches out and touches her knee. She makes a soft little sigh and places her hand lightly on his. "She's forgiven me," he thinks. But the woman's soft brown eyes are fixed on their daughter up at the cabin. The woman waves and calls out to her and as she does this the man feels a wave of jealousy that cuts across his chest like an electric jolt.)

Hi sugar!

(The daughter waves back. She looks disoriented by the sunlight shimmering off the water. She crosses her arms on her chest as though she's caught a sudden chill, steps over the broken cereal bowl, and heads down the stone path toward her parents. The man withdraws his hand from his wife's knee.)

She's a sleepy girl.

Skinny.

Yes. Very tall and skinny.

(The dogs rush up the path to greet the daughter but she pushes them off and keeps walking with her arms still crossed on her chest. Her mouth turns down and she twists her hips at the dogs as they keep dancing around her.)

She's always grumpy in the morning.

Very tall and grumpy.

Hi honey!

(The daughter makes a little sound of greeting and walks straight up on the dock to her father and sits on his lap. He kisses her on the neck. She puts her arm around his shoulder. The woman speaks.)

What's your brother doing?

He's crying.

What's he crying about?

I don't know. He's always crying.

He's not always crying.

Almost always. Who broke that bowl up there anyway?

Your brother.

Oh.

That's probably what he's crying about.

(The woman tosses the last of her cold coffee into the lake and shakes her cup dry. She stands and tightens the sash of her bathrobe. She stares up the hill at the cabin.)

I better go up and see. Looks like he's having a tough morning.

He's all right.

I'll be back. You want more coffee?

I'm fine.

(The woman leaves. The dogs join up with her now and swirl all around her legs as she heads back up the hill. The daughter rests her head on her father's chest. She stares at the flat dark water; the spot where her mother's coffee is still slowly sinking in a light brown cloud. She speaks to her father with dreamy eyes.)

Why's he always crying, Dad?

I don't know. He doesn't cry that much, does he?

Seems like he's always crying. He cries about everything.

He's all right.

(Another long pause. A frog jumps in the reeds. The daughter closes her

eyes as though she wants to return to sleep.)

Dad, do we really have to go to France?

France? Who told you we were going to France?

Mom. Mom said we were going to France.

(The screen door opens and slams as the woman enters the cabin. The loon pops up with a small silver fish twitching in its beak. Nobody sees this. The man gently strokes his daughter's hair. Suddenly he needs to stand up but the weight of his daughter is holding him down.)

Just a second, honey. I'll be right back, all right?

What's wrong?

Nothing's wrong. I just need to talk to your mother a second. I'll be right back. You just wait here.

Where are you going?

I'll be right back.

(He leaves his daughter sitting alone in the orange lawn chair and sprints back up the stone path to the cabin. His heart is thumping. Some old terror is rushing through him that he doesn't understand. The screen door slams behind him as he enters the kitchen. His wife is standing by the table with her back to him, stroking the hair of their son. The boy is sitting at the table digging into a fresh bowl of cereal. She turns to her husband but keeps stroking the soft hair of her son. The man goes

to her and holds her around the waist. She turns into him and they embrace. They kiss for a very long time; a long deep kiss like the way they used to before the children arrived. The boy keeps slurping his cereal, not looking up. He's not crying now. The crunching of Cheerios is the only sound. Then the clank of the spoon on the bowl. The man and woman stop kissing. He speaks.)

"Don't go to France," is what he says.

CONVULSION

If she could just see me now, she'd be sure to love me, I'll bet. I'll bet she would. How could she not? Look at me. Look at me now. How I am. If she could just see me like this—waiting for her, hours early, way before she's due; watching for any sign or sound of her. She'd see how eager I was. She'd see this desperation in my chest. If she could just see me now, from a distance, without me knowing she's watching, she'd see me as I really am. How could she not have some feeling toward me then? Some—but maybe not. Maybe that's—I mean, maybe there's some repulsion in something like that. I don't know how that works exactly but—maybe there's a—a revulsion of some kind when someone is too eager—too needful, too needy. I don't know. Some—convulsion. No. No, that's not— That's not it. That's not even a word is it? "Convulse." If she could just remember that one time, when was it—that one time back in Knoxville when we were kissing on the train; that long long kiss we had—saying good-bye—and the train suddenly took off from the station but I wasn't supposed to be going with her; I mean, that's why we were saying good-bye, thinking we weren't going to see each other again for a long, long time and we were locked in this long—just kissing and kissing and suddenly the train was moving and there was no way I could get off. Trees and houses were flashing by. So they dumped me at the next station, which was miles down the track, and there I was, waiting for hours for the next train back—I mean, if she could have seen me then, just standing there waiting, she'd—she'd be sure to love me. I mean, how could she not have some—I don't know. I don't know what causes that to happen— that connection—anymore. If there ever was one.

AN UNFAIR QUESTION

I was the one who volunteered to go hunt down more basil for the party. My wife very pointedly held the last tiny clump of it under my nose so I got the full authentic aroma, the shape and color of the leaves, as though I might confuse it somehow with mint or watercress. "Fresh basil. Make sure it's fresh," she stressed. "They have it up at Rainbow Foods, I think. That's probably the only place you'll find it on a Sunday." She smiled and turned back into the fray of family women chopping garlic, boiling rice, and clanging pots and pans around. I was glad to have an excuse to get out of there and away from all the frantic urgency of guests arriving. I can't even remember now what the celebration was all about. It wasn't a death and it wasn't a wedding. I remember that much.

I was looking forward to the ride alone in the car, up the long hill to Rainbow Foods—a twenty-four-hour supermarket on the edge of town in one of those early-sixties malls that had been made obsolete by newer, more strategically placed malls. I liked the wide, maple-canopied Midwestern streets where the twenty-five-mph speed limit was accepted as though it were part of the Lutheran credo and where if you had the audacity actually to pass anyone you were honked at vigorously but rarely given the finger. Minnesota pedestrians tended to stare right into your car as you passed, studying every inch of your face with an almost desperate expectation of finding something—some clue in the eyes of a total stranger. What could they possibly be looking for? I don't know any other region of the country where they stare into your car with such bewilderment. Maybe it comes from surviving too many long winters and lutefisk church buffets.

I parked in the huge, almost empty parking lot skirting Rainbow Foods, a parking lot that at one time must have held high hopes. Now there were only three pathetic beater cars bunched together, probably employee-owned, real rattletrap Minnesota cars with the rusted-out scars of bitter blizzards and salted roads. A kid with a long green apron and a backward baseball cap was pushing a line of shopping carts, snaking them back toward the electric doors of Rainbow Foods. I turned the ignition off and watched him heave his wafer-thin body against the weight of the carts, inching them past all the abandoned, out-of-business storefronts: The Pet Palace, Nora's Nails, 24 Hour Developing. The plate-glass windows of each store were blocked out halfway up with brown butcher paper, I guess to keep people from looking in at all the emptiness. I got out and squeezed the button on my remote-control door lock. This is an affectation I'd long despised in other drivers, but now I find myself not only doing it but enjoying the sensation of detached authority it gives me. I especially enjoy it when the car beeps and blinks back at you, confirming that everything is locked and secure. I stood there for a long while in that almost empty parking lot, just facing the car door and pushing the button over and over, watching the lights blink and listening to the horn honk, until I noticed that the kid pushing the carts had stopped and was staring at me as though I might be dangerous. I smiled and pointed my remote-control button in his direction. He immediately fled with his train of carts, toward the doors of Rainbow Foods. A sudden great feeling of freedom and aloneness swept over me. I stared out at the deep-gray swirls of clouds against the setting sun. The prairie wind was whipping a rope on the tall aluminum flagpole, making a rhythmic clanking while, at the top, a gigantic American flag popped and snarled like it was trying to bite itself in the ass. A V of geese slid silently across the long silver shelf of clouds, silhouetted against the sunset. Usually, they make that frantic honking, as though pleading with some unseen force to get them safely back down to earth, but these were completely silent. I couldn't even hear the snap of their wings as they passed over.

I went through the electric doors and the air-conditioning blasted me in the chest. There was no one in the place except for the kid with the green apron, who was now spraying the carrots and bok choy with a fine mist from a water wand. He didn't see me. I started hunting for basil. There was no basil. There was spinach and parsley and turnips and endive and celery, but no basil. I made a special double check, going back through the racks of dripping colorful vegetables, wishing I could be transported to some of the places where they'd originated, like Gilroy, California—"Garlic Capital of the World." I walked over to the kid with the apron. He was still waving the water wand back and forth over the parsnips. The gentle mist hit me in the face and filled me with a great sense of joy. I don't know why. Pure joy. "Seen any basil?" I asked the kid. He turned and stared at me vacantly while he continued to wave the wand around. The mist floated up between us.

"What's basil?" he said.

"It's green; small leaf—very distinctive smell. Looks like it could be mint or watercress, but it's not."

"Never heard of it," he said. I left him standing there holding his wand. I could feel his gaze following me. He was alone in that cavernous supermarket with me, and I could have been anyone. A maniac maybe—searching for basil. I gave it up.

Back at the house, the party is now in full swing. Balloons hang from the front gate. The dogs have been locked in the garage, whining and clawing desperately at the door. Why they crave human attention is beyond me. People are already milling around the lawn holding drinks, paper plates, and napkins out in front of them. You can tell right away which ones have developed a party technique for handling plates and drinks and which ones are awkward about it. A couple smile at me, but I don't recognize them. I sneak in the back door and wind my way through the loud crowd to the kitchen. "No basil!" I report to the women at large, who are now very busy with pies and bread.

"That's all right, we don't need it now," one of them says, and offers me a big wooden spoonful of green pasta sauce out of the blender.

"Tastes just like basil," I say.

"It *is* basil," one of them giggles.

"Oh, so you didn't need basil, then?"

"No, I guess not. We seem to have found some."

"Oh, good," I say. Now I start recognizing faces around me but can't put any names to them. Relatives of my wife. Country faces. Some of whom have even fewer social skills than myself. I feel a strange empathy with these weathered northern men, with their huge knuckled hands and gentle ice-blue eyes. Even so, it makes it no easier to chat with them. There is a woman from New York who stands out from all the Midwesterners in her solid-black scary outfit with lace-up combat boots and shorn matching black hair. She has an anguished, perplexed look, as if she's done way too much time in psychotherapy. She's going on and on about how she got lost in her rental car trying to find her way out here from the Minneapolis–St. Paul airport. She seems to have a great appetite for engaging people in her smallest dilemmas and turning them into some huge dramatic deal.

Finally, I recognize a woman from Montana, a friend of my wife's sister, who I've always found fairly easy to talk to, mainly because she'll talk about anything that pops into her head, from Shakespeare to Christmas pudding. She finds everything "fascinating" and "wonderful." I veer toward her, hoping I can engage her before someone else does, and, sure enough, in less than a minute she is asking me about guns—not my favorite subject, but it beats Bush-bashing or Tiger Woods–fawning, which seem to be the two main topics in the room. She is concerned about a recent string of assaults on single women in the area of St. Paul she's just moved into and is wondering if maybe now is the time to consider carrying a side arm. I find it hard to believe that anyone could get assaulted in St. Paul, but what do I know? I never go into the cities. I try to discourage the woman from Montana from carrying a weapon at all, with the usual caution that it could be used against her. Instead, I recommend she pick up a .410 shotgun for household protection, just in case some idiot followed her home and busted down her door. "You can't miss with a .410," I tell her. "It's light. It's fast. And you can shoot from the hip." She smiles. She likes the Western connotation. She asks me if I own one and I tell her yes, but it's not for sale. She asks if she can see it so she at least knows what a .410 looks like. "Well, they're all down in the basement in a big shipping crate," I tell her. "I never unpacked them since we moved from Virginia."

"Oh, so you mean we can't see them, then?" she says, acting deeply disappointed. I'm surprised she could attach so much emotion to a .410 so quickly.

"No, we could go down there, I guess. I can see if I could dig them out."

"You could? That would be fantastic!" We head down to the basement, weaving through the kitchen, now packed with teenage girls, friends of my daughter; polka-dot bandannas and Birkenstocks— very athletic, sunburned, take-no-shit-from-men type of girls. My daughter gives me a loving pat on the head as we go by. It reminds me I'm a father and at the same time makes me feel slightly childlike.

It's been five years since I even looked at the tall shipping crate where the shotguns and rifles are packed away. I stopped hunting after we moved here, mainly because in the Midwest it's illegal to hunt deer with a rifle and I find the idea of maiming one with a shotgun slug and having him drag off into the woods and slowly bleed to death the height of idiocy. I spot the crate in a dark, moldy corner behind the boiler and rummage around through the long, heavy barrels wrapped in padded butcher paper and sealed up with masking tape. The woman from Montana is right behind me, breathing heavily. "You can tell just by the feel of them which one is which?" she asks me.

"Yes, well, the .410 has a very skinny barrel, almost like a .22. Very light. Skinnier than a 20-gauge," I tell her.

"So you know every gun in there just by the feel of the barrel? That's incredible!" she says.

"Not really," I say. "Like, for instance, this one here—I know this is a .270 by the scope. See?" She reaches out and gingerly touches the bulge under the paper.

"Oh," she says. "I see. So the .410 doesn't have a scope, then? Is that the idea?"

"Right. The .410's a shotgun. A small shotgun. This is a rifle."

"Oh, so there's a difference between a shotgun and a rifle?" she says.

It suddenly feels like I've been duped. Upstairs the party is going full tilt and the kids have cranked up Moby on the speakers and there's a sudden thunderous cacophony of voices all speaking simultaneously and shrieking to be heard over the swelling music and something is so funny that it sounds as though somebody had just held up a cue card. What am I doing down here? Finally, I find the skinny .410 and strip the paper off it and hoist it out of the packing crate.

"Oh, it looks just like a toy gun!" she says, and backs away while I crack the slim barrel and make sure it's empty. "Can I hold it?" she says.

"Sure," I say, and hand it over to her after I close the barrel with a snap. She holds it up to her shoulder so awkwardly that I wonder if she's ever been anywhere near Montana. She squints one eye very tightly, which is something you never have to do with a shotgun, and points the gun at the washing machine.

"Have you killed things with this?" she says, sort of wistfully.

"Yes. Yes, I have," I say.

"Really? What have you killed?" she says, and swings the barrel recklessly toward the water-heating tank.

"Varmints," I say. "Mostly varmints."

"Varmints? Really? What kind of varmints?" she says.

"Rats, birds, and snakes."

"Birds? Birds aren't varmints," she says, opening her eye. Her gaze seems out of focus.

"Starlings are," I say.

"Starlings?"

"Yeah, that's right. Starlings."

"But aren't they just innocent birds like you'd have in the yard or something?" she says. Now she's aiming the gun at the bare lightbulbs in the ceiling and pretending to pull the trigger and making little explosion sounds. I find this very disturbing for some reason.

"No—starlings are horrible stinky birds," I say. "Don't you know about starlings? In Virginia, we used to have outbreaks of them."

"Outbreaks?" She giggles.

"Yes. That's right. Outbreaks. That's exactly what they were—starling outbreaks. They'd nest in the chimneys, and then hatch their babies in the spring. The babies would fly down into the bedroom and shit all over the rugs and curtains and the bedspread."

"Why would they fly down into the bedroom?" she asks, holding the stock of the shotgun tight up against her jaw.

"What?" I say.

"Why would the baby starlings fly down into the bedroom instead of flying up the chimney and out into the sky?"

"Because baby birds, when they hatch, usually fall before they fly. Haven't you noticed that up in Montana?"

"Where?" she says.

"Montana. Isn't that where you said you were from?"

"Oh, yeah—Montana. Right. But I never noticed baby birds falling up there."

"Maybe you weren't paying very close attention to the seasons," I say.

"So you had to actually shoot these little baby starlings in Virginia because they were falling into your bedroom and making a mess?"

"That's right."

"Couldn't you have just opened a window and let them fly out?"

"Starlings are very stupid birds," I tell her.

"They wouldn't fly out?"

"That's right. They'd crash into the window and then flop around on the floor, bleeding all over everything and twittering their heads off."

"Couldn't you just shoosh them out with a broom or something?"

"No. No, I couldn't just 'shoosh' them out with a broom."

"Why not?"

"Because I wanted to see them die! That's why not. I wanted to see them splattered against the Colonial wallpaper and the embroidered curtains. I wanted to see their little feathers fluttering around through the dusty air of the Old Dominion."

"That's horrible!" she says. "You'd just shoot them?"

"Yes. I'd get drunk on red wine and lie in bed with that .410 across my lap and smoke Camels and I'd wait for them."

"Innocent baby birds?" She gives me some kind of Greenpeace stare, as though she can't believe she could have so misjudged me.

"Yeah. I'd lie there sometimes for hours, waiting and drinking Italian red wine, and I'd hear them making this god-awful tweetering sound up in the chimney, which meant their stupid mother had come to feed them. They'd get all frantic and shrieking like. And then finally one of them would fall down in the fireplace, thrashing around in the ashes."

"That's terrible," she says. "And you'd just lie there watching the poor little thing? And you wouldn't even try to help it?"

"Help it? I was there to kill it! Why would I want to help it?"

"Because— Because that's what people— That's what human beings are supposed to—" She gets so flustered she can't go on.

"I'd watch it whipping its naked wings around, trying to fly in circles through the ashes until it finally flopped out onto the rug. It'd lie there dazed for a while, gasping for air and looking all around with its ugly little yellow eye, wondering where in the hell it had fallen and what had happened to its cozy nest with all its little brothers and sisters, and then, finally, it would have rested enough to prop itself up on its wobbly chicken-looking legs and fly straight up and come crashing straight down again."

"That's just awful! You're making this up," she says, and sets the .410 down on top of the washing machine and turns as though to go back to the party upstairs, but I'm blocking her way now.

"It would keep making these disastrous test flights like that, flying straight up and straight down until—"

"I don't really want to hear any more about this," she says, and tries to push past me.

"Until finally it would make one big explosive effort and hit the ceiling, then start thrashing, looking for something to hang on to, something to break its fall—and usually that was one of our curtains."

"Our?" she says. "Oh, so you were living with someone then? You weren't alone?" She seems almost relieved at the idea.

"I was alone," I say. "I was drinking Italian red wine and I was very much alone!"

"Oh," she says. "I think maybe I'll just go back upstairs and see if—" I make a quick move over to the washing machine and grab the gun. I crack the barrel open.

"What are you doing?" she says. I start going through the packing crate, looking for shells to fit the gun, talking the whole time, telling her the starling story in a very level narrator-type voice. A voice like Robert Stack's.

"So I keep watching the dumb thing. I keep my eye on him.

106

He's just sitting up there on the curtain rod breathing real hard, his heart thumping away. Just hanging on to the curtain for dear life. And I've had about two bottles of wine by now. Brunello di Montalcino. Aged in oak. Have you ever tried it?" I ask her.

"I don't drink wine," she says, and her face looks very grim and ashen. I finally find the green box of slim .410 shells and open it. I take one out and slip it into the open chamber, then snap the barrel shut.

"Well, I was unhappy back then, see. I was very unhappy, and drinking that stuff made me feel good. It didn't make me feel happy, it just made me feel all right about myself. You know what I mean? Does that make sense to you?" She nods. "It felt all right to be laid up way out in the deep country all by myself with a .410 across my lap, shit-faced drunk, listening to cicadas, chain-smoking, and shooting starlings off the curtains in my bedroom until three in the morning. I never could have predicted it, that's for sure. I never saw the situation coming. Just like this—just like this one right here."

"What do you mean?" she says.

"This. No way to predict this. That I'd be down here in the basement showing you a gun while there's a party going on upstairs, and talking about the past."

"I think I'll just go on back up and—" She gasps when I raise the gun up over her head and train it on a can of yellow tennis balls high up on the shelf behind her. She freezes and starts to tremble a little.

"I'm not going to shoot you," I say. She giggles and makes a little spitting sound.

"Well, I hope not!" she says. "Why would you want to shoot me?"

"I don't," I say. "I don't want to shoot you."

"Isn't this a little dangerous?"

"What?" I say, holding the .410 above her head, aimed right at the can of tennis balls.

"Pointing a loaded gun at somebody."

"I'm not pointing it at you. I'm pointing it at that can of balls."

"But it's in my direction," she says.

"No, it isn't. This is in your direction, see? Right here." And I lower the barrel so it's point-blank right in the middle of her breastbone. Now she screams. It's one of those extremely shrill horror-movie-type screams. The party goes silent upstairs. Not a voice can be heard. The music stops. You can't even hear the dogs whining anymore. The woman from Montana starts shaking her head, twitching it from side to side, and is now making a muffled squealing sound. "Stop twitching," I tell her, with the barrel of the gun still leveled at her chest. She stops. "You're not from Montana, are you? Tell the truth." She closes her eyes and squeezes them so hard that tiny tears burst out from the corners, looking more like sweat than tears. "Tell the truth!" She shakes her head. I start whispering to her for some reason. "I was very, very unhappy back then, when I was shooting starlings in my bedroom. Have you ever been very, very unhappy?" She nods vigorously. "What were you very, very unhappy about?" I ask her. She just shakes her head and keeps smothering her mouth with both hands. "I wasn't sure what it was, either," I say. "I never could quite put my finger on it. It's probably an unfair question, don't you think? To ask someone why they're very, very unhappy?" She nods frantically. My daughter's voice comes from the top of the basement staircase.

"Dad? Are you all right down there?"

"Yes," I say. "I'm fine."

A FRIGHTENING SEIZURE

Back then, just before he'd run off, the main thing that had struck the two kids as strange about their father's behavior was not so much when he set the raw brown egg down on the breakfast counter between their bowls of fruit salad and smashed it with his fist so that it sprayed all over the telephone and their paper bag lunches, but more the way he convulsed into maniacal laughter as he went about cleaning the whole mess up. It was a frightening seizure that gathered such rapid momentum they could see deep in their father's eyes the terrible self-doubt that he might not return from it; that he might very easily get swept down into such twisted currents of totally conflicting emotions he would not only not recognize those closest and dearest to him but, more importantly, he would no longer recognize himself. This was an instinctive, unspoken revelation in both children and marked the very beginnings of their sense of what it might mean to be totally on their own. Over the years, they had grown used to their father's screwy bursts of exuberance where he'd, quite suddenly, seem to succumb to some adolescent whim like deliberately swerving into a closed-off construction lane on the highway in order to knock over all the little plastic orange witch hats, shrieking with glee and pounding the steering wheel until his knuckles bled. Or the time he jumped out of the green canoe into the James River when they were very little and thrashed around, pretending to drown. There was always some sense of controlled vaudeville about these acts and, in fact, even at an early age, the kids had the impression that their father was actually performing for them; showing off. They had no idea why. For the most part, they found him quite funny and entertaining. It wasn't until their teenage years that they began to notice a distinct difference in his digressions. The difference was marked by the degree to which he was able to distance himself from his antics. More and more it seemed that he would take the plunge and get swallowed up, lost in some inner reaction always belied by his eyes. They could see the eyes turning to terror. That was never a factor in their younger days. No matter how wild their father's choices might have been, he always seemed to be enjoying himself. Now there was a definite turning point. The laughter shifted into a cackle; a kind of staccato rampage that was no longer connected to anything funny. Smashing the egg wasn't all that funny to begin with; shocking maybe but not funny. Not funny like a comedy anyway, and it was even interfering with their homework and their incoming phone calls. They left the kitchen with their books and papers and took the telephone with them. Their father was down on his hands and knees at this point with wet paper towels and the water running in the sink and the laughter still attacking him in rolling spurts. The kids went upstairs and shut themselves up in their rooms; turned their radios on to hip-hop stations and dialed the volume up trying to drown out the sounds coming from the kitchen below. Sounds which were now deeply disturbing and not resembling laughter at all anymore but more like wailing or mourning or wounded animal noises that went on and on and then suddenly stopped in short blank silences. Silences where both the kids would turn their radios way down to listen for how he was progressing, then turn them back up again with the next explosion. Slowly, the silences began to outweigh the hysteria until there was nothing at all coming from the kitchen. The kids listened to the back door thump very softly and then the sound of the Buick turning over. They heard the tires crunching through the gravel as it backed down the driveway and the gears shifting when the gravel turned to blacktop. They heard the big engine move off into the night and fade away to a hum that sounded like vast empty space. A space not even their radios could protect them from. This was several years ago and they haven't seen him since.

Today, they both saw someone who looked a whole lot like their father sneaking into the post office to get his mail, and when they asked their mother about it, why he was going around in disguise, dressed up as an old man, she said, "That's no disguise. That's him. He got old fast."

TINNITUS

Palmer? It's me again. I've arrived for the night. It's about—oh, eight-thirty, nine or so. Quit the road a little early on account of the old spine was starting to give me trouble and I couldn't keep my mind on the straight and narrow; not to mention that chronic ringing in my left ear I told you about. I've plunked down in Normal, Illinois, at a Best Western just off exit 8; room number 119, I think it is—no wait a second—yeah, 119. Had to check the key. Place is called "The Normal Midwesterner." Some joke. I've registered under the name "Guy Talmer," Two Creek, Virginia—on account of the phony plates. Sounds a little fruity but the fella behind the counter didn't even blink. I don't even think they read the names anymore these days. Used the American Express, like you said. No way they can make any links back to you. It's still colder than bloody blue Jesus; minus forty when I left St. Paul and no sign of a letup. Can't wait to hit warmer climes down south, although Nick tells me it's in the teens in Lexington. Should pull in there tomorrow sometime around six, I reckon, maybe earlier, depends on traffic. So far the Interstate's clean and frosty but no ice. Highway Department's been on the ball with the plowing. Shoulda seen the vapors swirling across the blacktop like you'd think you were on Mars or something. Real unfriendly out there. Probably won't get out to see your mare until Thursday or Friday but she should hold up until then. I'll send you my assessment right away. Fax or phone, you'll hear from me the second I give her the once-over. I assume your lawyer talked to the vet since I last saw you, but just to bring you up to date: all the wheels are coming off her now. She's foundered bad in the off right fore and there's profuse seepage all along the coronet band. I suppose this is a natural result of supporting all the weight off her amputated leg. In any case, Doc Roxsin has inserted pins to relieve some of the pressure of the laminitus and switched her to a heavier dose of IV bute to thwart the pain and take the swelling down. I've double-checked with the insurance company and they're ready to honor the claim anytime you give the go-ahead to put the mare down. All this was done anonymous of course. The check will be sent directly to me in the subcompany name and then I'll deposit it in whatever account you designate, either Stateside or abroad. Just send me the code number and details. Actually, they can't believe we're trying to save the mare. They've had claims on far lesser injuries where the animal was dropped within twenty-four hours. This has been a week and a half now since she snapped her cannon and we're still coaxing her along. They must think we're some kind of humanitarian heroes or something. I've already given you my opinion on this situation, but if you want to prolong her life long enough to save the foal she's carrying, that's certainly your decision. She's your mare after all. There's a risk involved there too, of course. The foal could be premature and die from the induced labor or various other complications that go hand in hand with a mare under duress. For my money, there's no reason to cause the mare more suffering than she's already been through. She's gone way past the call of duty and given her all on the racetrack. I just hate to see her suffer. It's true, the foal might turn out to be a genuine racehorse given her pedigree and the sire's history of producing solid runners, but sometimes it's hard to weigh these things against the reality of pain. I've got the Weather Channel on here and you wouldn't believe the monster that's heading up from the Gulf: ice, snow, sleet, driving winds, and minus zero! What in the world is going on? Feels like the wrath of God or something. Anyhow, it'll be good just to get back in the old bluegrass again. More later.

WED., 2/2—LEXINGTON, KY.

Palmer—Can't seem to catch you in but I hope you received last night's phone mail. Good thing I got it off to you when I did because I had a real rough night's sleep. Woke up three or four times at the witching hour to the sounds of what at first I thought was murder. Turned out to be some crazy pair screwing their brains out in the room next door. They must line the beds up in Normal head to head against those Sheetrock walls and all night the thumping and moaning was beyond belief. I mean this gal must've not had any for a good year or two by the way she was carrying on. "Yes! Yes! Give it to me! Oh, yes! Fuck me, Jesus! Fuck me! Fuck me!" Uh-oh, I hope this doesn't get listened to by some innocent secretary or other. Anyhow, I'm all checked into Lexington now under "Lyle Maybry." Swapped over to the MasterCard, just in case. Thought it might be safer if they happen to put a tracer on that Normal address. Hope you don't mind. My ear's ringing real bad tonight so I thought I'd run out to the clinic first thing in the morning and check the mare. Nothing much I could do tonight anyhow as far as new information since only the night watchman's on duty there. I've been keeping in touch with Doc Roxsin and he assures me the mare's hanging tough as best she can, although time is running out fast. I just can't believe this ear of mine. Constant buzzing like some kind of radio interference. It's never bothered me like this before. Must be the direct result of all those years of dove shooting, back before they ever dreamed up earplugs. Most days I don't even notice it but lately it's been a real constant companion. Probably put the whole thing down to age. All the parts are wearing thin. By the way, did you notice Arcaro passed away? Now there's a real milestone. Never forget his Triple Crown year on Citation. Nineteen forty-eight, I think it was. Old "Banana Nose." Smooth as silk. Feels strange now to be back down here in hard-boot country again. I was really looking forward to it but now that I'm here I catch the blues. Funny how that happens. Start reminiscing in my head, I guess. All those years ago when I first met Martha. It was right here at Keeneland, 1959. Hard to believe. You remember, Palmer—you were the one who dared me to ask her out for a highball and steak. That was just the beginning. Twenty-two years of pure hell. Actually, I miss her, truth be known. I don't know why. Maybe too much road. I'll keep trying to get through. If we don't hook up you can always leave a message here at the desk. Remember, it's "Lyle Maybry" now. I lose track myself.

THURS., 2/3—LEXINGTON, KY.

Palmer! Where the hell are you? I need some contact ASAP! I've been out to check the mare and we've decided to go ahead and induce her now, since she's really failing bad. The foal will be two weeks premature but at this point there's no other option. I'm on a direct beeper now to the clinic, calling you from a booth off Ironworks Pike on the Transmedia card, under the name "Filson." Can't remember the code right now. Here's the lowdown and I need an answer quick; the second this mare goes into labor they're going to buzz me and I'll have to drop this phone and beat it back to the clinic. What I need from you is the okay to put the mare down as soon as she foals. They can't do it without the registered owner's permission. Send me some kind of verification of this right away. Most urgent! I'm going back there now to assist the foaling and I've made it clear to all the personnel that I want the mare to nuzzle the colt and mother up to it as much as she's able to before we destroy her. I've always felt that's important for the baby down the road. They seem to remember that in deep stretch when the whip comes down. I've arranged for a good nurse mare to be brought in off a reputable farm. None of these floaters. She should be on her way over to the clinic now. I'll go check her out and make sure her bag's clean and full and see what kind of temperament she's got on her. This clinic is top-notch, Palmer, and your mare is getting all the attention she deserves. It's just kind of a heartbreaker to see her go down like this. She's such a lovely thing and pure hickory through and through. Please respond the second you get this message. The clock is running out.

THURS., 2/3—LATER

Palmer—well, congratulations! You've got a brand-new colt. Big, strapping, scopey chestnut. We had to foal the mare standing up and pretty much pull the baby throughout, even though he was in the diving position. He started out real strong, then dropped off suddenly to where we thought we might lose him. We boosted him with shots to keep him going and I think he's going to make it now. It'll take a while to get him up and test him on the nurse mare so we're not quite out of the woods yet. Time will tell. The mare was a real champ through the whole ordeal, showed the same class she had on the racetrack, but I finally had to give the nod to let her go. I told another little fib and claimed I had power of attorney but had left the notary sheet back at the motel. I've become a professional liar these days. All the vets went along with it since they could see this was the only route to go for her in the sad condition she was in. Her leg was starting to stink real bad from infection setting in and she was just sinking in every direction. Doc Roxsin put in a strong appeal to keep the mare alive for the sake of continuing his experimental work on the amputation but I just couldn't justify it; seeing her suffer like that. What kind of life was she going to have hobbling around on three legs in some padded stall somewhere? So, what's done is done. Hopefully this colt will make it through the tunnel and win you some big-stakes money down the road. I hope all this doesn't upset you too much, but there was really nothing else I could do, given the circumstances and not getting any word from you. I hope to Christ you get these messages soon. I have no earthly clue where you are or how to get ahold of you. Even if there's a secretary there who's minding the store, maybe she could get back to me and verify that all this is getting through to you. I don't know what else to do. First thing tomorrow morning I'll contact the agent at the insurance company and let them know we destroyed the mare. I'm sure there'll be no problems with the check. It's way too late to get ahold of them now—1:30 a.m. here. Think I'll head on down to Barclay's and have a Maker's on the rocks; maybe two. Haven't touched the stuff in months but this whole thing has really shook me some. I just hate to see an animal go through that. Especially one like her. She was a real peach. My ear's gone completely berserk now and the static has escalated into a high moan like some kind of distant tornado warning. Hope it's not an omen. I'll be in touch. As always—

THE STOUT OF HEART

"Can you please go up and just talk to him? That's all I'm asking," she says to me in that pleading little-girl voice that I recognize from long ago.

"What's he doing up there?"

"He's buried in those catalogues again. It's that time of year when they send him the catalogues. A whole boxful arrives and he carries them up there like they're alive or something. He goes in his room and he won't come out. For days he's been up there. A week now at least."

"A week?"

"A week solid. Smoking. That's all he does since he quit drinking. Smokes and coughs. The kids have tried to bring him sandwiches but he won't eat. He won't answer them or anything. Won't even open the door."

"He's not dead, is he?"

"Oh, that's very funny. I thought you came to help." And with this she starts to break down and tremble around the corners of her voluptuous mouth. The mouth, too, is something I remember. Something I'll never forget. I pat her shoulder but she pulls away fast, hiding her face.

"I'll go up."

"Good," she says, and moves to the sink with purpose, like she's about to start a major cleanup. "If he lets you in ask him how long he thinks this will go on. It's not for me I'm asking. It's for the kids."

"I'll ask him."

"Good. Just ask him how long he thinks we can stand this." She swallows hard on the last word and flips the water on full blast so the splashing covers her sobs.

I shuffle up the stairs past photos of their kids in soccer gear and beaming smiles. Past fishing scenes and better days. At the landing I can smell his smoke. I follow it down the hall to his door with a horseshoe hook on it suspending raincoats, belts, and a dark wool vest. I knock. No answer. "Reese?" I say to the door. "Reese, it's me, Jamey. You in there?" I hear a chair slide across the floorboards. Silence. I hear him slowly stand. A cough. He moves to the door and stops. I can hear him breathing on the other side. He's very close. "Reese? Lemme in, okay? I wanna talk to you."

"Door's open." His voice comes soft and broken like he hasn't used it for a while; almost boyish. I hear him return to his chair and sit. As I crack the door the acrid stench of Lucky Strikes hits me full in the face. There's a blue-gray haze layering the room from floor to ceiling. I can see him across the fog, sitting at his desk with his back to me. It's a tiny room. One whole wall devoted to books. The other three crammed with framed photos of racehorses, jockeys, mares and foals grazing emerald fields. One window above his typewriter with a view through venetian blinds to garage roofs gleaming in the crisp October light. Orange maple leaves sail downward and disappear. His back stays to me. His hair has gray wings now that wrap around the base of his neck. A cigarette smolders from a carved teakwood ashtray in the shape of some Polynesian princess sitting on a sea turtle. He doesn't turn around. He doesn't move. Stacks of pedigree reference books and pumpkin-colored horse sale catalogues surround him almost shoulder high, in a paper bunker. "Did Rena put you up to this?" he says after I've stood there awhile, staring at the back of his head.

"Put me up to what?"

"Close the door," he says. I follow his directions and now he turns to see me, scraping his chair around like one of those old men you weren't supposed to bust in on when you were a kid and they were playing cards without women. I can hear the water being turned off downstairs and I imagine Rena listening. I picture her drying her soft hands at the foot of the stairs and straining to hear some clue. "I'd offer you a buzz but I'm on the wagon," he says.

"Me too," I say.

"Imagine that. The two of us? Ten years ago we'd be shit-faced and down the road."

"Most likely."

"I've found the source," he says without a beat.

"The what?"

"The factory. A taproot mare. Blue Hen. Right here!" He slaps the shortest stack of catalogues, causing ashes to billow up between the thighs of the Polynesian princess. "Had to weed her out from four thousand two hundred and sixty-one hip numbers but here she is!" He scrapes the chair back toward his desk, wets his thumb, and slashes his way through dog-eared pages landing on hip number 773. "There!" he says, and leans back satisfied, inviting my inspection of the pedigree. I go along with it out of deference and start fishing for my glasses. "Have you ever seen anything like it?" he says. "Not a hole in it through four generations. Solid gold."

"Yeah, looks good," I say.

"Good? Good! Have you ever seen 'Hay Patcher' that close up?

When's the last time you saw 'Hay Patcher' as the second dam? Not for a good long while, I'll tell ya."

"What's a mare like this go for these days?"

"I'm gonna steal her for a ham sandwich. Look who she's bred to." My stinging eyes track down the page to a covering sire I've never heard of.

" 'Traekon'? Who's 'Traekon'?"

"Exactly. That's what I'm saying. Some allowance piece of shit out of Uruguay or something. A pure plodder. Couldn't beat a fat man uphill."

"Aren't you gonna have a hard time selling the foal back then?"

"The foal? I'm not in it for the foal, man! Are you crazy? I'm in it for the long haul. Mares like this are for the stout of heart. The future. The *History of the Turf* books!"

"I thought you were supposed to be a little short on change these days, Reese."

"Who told you that? Oh, the exes you mean?"

"Well—"

"Yeah. News is out, I guess. They've finally tapped me. I've got other resources, though. Kentucky's full of loopholes. Deals can be made, believe you me. Deals can be made."

"How many extra kids are you supporting now?"

"Too goddamn many! Half of 'em aren't even mine to begin with but I haven't got the funds to fight it." Now he closes off again; lights another Lucky and burrows into his reference books, blowing smoke across the pages.

"Rena kinda wants to know how long you're gonna stay up here, Reese."

"Rena. That's what I figured. She called you, right?"

"No, she didn't call me."

"She called you, all right. I can tell by your demeanor."

"My demeanor?"

"Yeah. The way you come crawling in here sideways."

"You weren't even looking! You had your back to me."

"I could feel it. I've grown very sensitive to that kinda stuff over the years. Treachery and guile. I can feel it."

"Well, I didn't crawl. That's ridiculous."

"You slithered."

"Look—all she wants to know is how long. That's all."

"I haven't got the answer to that. As long as it takes." Now it's silent again. I'm drowned in his tight world. There's no way out. My eyes feel like they're bleeding from the smoke. I scan up to the wall of books and lock on titles: *Last Grass Frontier, The Wind Leaves No Shadow, These Were the Vaqueros, Production of Field Crops* by Wolfe and Kipps; an entire red set of *American Broodmare Records* with dark gaps where he's taken them down to devour statistics. In one of the gaps a Smith & Wesson Airweight .38 sits propped in a clip holster. I recognize it from long ago. Back when it used to make sudden appearances under parking lot lights and rubber bands snapped on crisp rolls of fifties. Another golden leaf sails past his window, disappearing.

"So, what're you thinking, you're gonna head down to Lexington and try and snag that mare? Is that it?"

"Wanna come along?" he says, turning to me with the cigarette drooping from a sly smile. "We could be down there and back in four days. Simple."

"What about the kids?"

"School."

"Rena then?"

"Rena?" He chuckles, then stifles a cough. "She doesn't need

122

me. Are you kidding? She hasn't needed me for a long, long time."
He retreats again to his gray pages.

"She's pretty upset right now."

"Upset."

"Seemed like it to me."

"You don't know her."

"I used to."

"Yeah, you did, didn't you." He slips the wet Lucky into the
ashtray and turns to me slow. "You knew her pretty good. I bet you
even have thoughts in your mind right now."

"Thoughts?" I say.

"Yeah, thoughts. Thoughts like, 'If she was still with me she
might be happy. She might be a whole different person than what
she is now. She might be raising *my* blond kids instead of his.'"

"I wasn't thinking anything like that."

"Yeah, you were. Don't gimme that. Something right along
those lines. What makes you think you wouldn't have messed up
the same way I did?"

"You haven't messed up, Reese."

"Don't gimme that condescending crap. You somehow think
you're just a little bit superior, don't ya? Always have."

"I'm not getting into this."

"Just a little bit superior in every department. Especially with
the chicks."

"All she wants to know is when you're coming down! That's
all." Silence again but this time he doesn't turn away. He stares
straight at me and slowly a smile of recognition pans across his
face.

"You actually believe that?" he says.

"What?"

"That's all she wants to know?"

"That's what she said."

"That's *not* all she wants to know."

"What then?"

"She wants to know where I've gone away to! That's what she wants to know. What country! What territory of the mind! What region of isolation! Women are very social animals. Don't you know that? This kind of business terrifies them!"

"Well, maybe you could explain it to her then."

"I can't explain this to her!" he says, suddenly exploding to his feet and knocking the massive *Stallion Register* off the corner of his desk. "Are you crazy? How could I explain this to her? How could I possibly explain how each and every name in one of these pedigrees means something to me? How just the sound 'Nasrullah' calls something up in me. His savage temperament. His unruly speed!"

"All right, take it easy, Reese. I don't need a lecture."

" 'Seattle Slew'! 'Storm Bird'! 'Native Dancer'! 'Silver Spoon'! How am I supposed to explain something like that!" He's charging around in tight circles now like a caged bear with me thrown out of the vortex up against the bookcase. "I can't explain how when I see 'Cool Mood' doubled up in the third generation my spine gets hot and tingly! How 'Dr. Fager,' 'Great Above,' and 'Aspidistra' share a common lock! What in the world am I supposed to do with that? She's got to know the history! The lineage! The perpetuity of the whole thing! She's lost without that! Totally lost!" He stops cold, panting for breath, as though suddenly revisiting his body after being absent for a long time. He looks across at me like I've just now arrived in his room.

"Well look, Reese—" I say. "What if you just took a little break now and then. You know—went down and talked to her once a day or something. Had coffee. Saw the kids a little." He stares at me for a while, still trying to get his breath back and squinting his eyes in an effort to decipher my words.

"*You* talk to her," he finally says, and returns to the familiarity of his chair. "I'm busy." He leans over and retrieves the *Stallion Register*, then thumps it back to its original corner. "Go on down and have a cup of coffee with her yourself. You must have a lot to chat about, you two. You can reminisce or something. Go down memory lane."

"So there's nothing you want me to tell her then?"

"Yeah. Yeah, there is. Tell her this—Tell her that some fine day I will reemerge. I will come back into the light of day!"

"All right," I say as I watch him grab his cigarette and dissolve back into his books. I cross back to the door and grab the handle. "Well look, it's been good seeing you again, Reese." I watch his spine straighten up slightly and the back of his head tilts in my direction.

"We could drive down there, you know," he says in the soft voice I heard before I entered. "Just the two of us. Just like the old days. Kentucky. There's nothin' stopping us. Think about it."

"I've pretty much lost touch with that world."

"Still there. Still hummin' right along. No end to the funny money."

"I'd be like a fish outta water now, Reese."

"Yeah. Yeah, you probably would."

"Well, good luck with that mare. I hope you get her."

"Oh, I'll get her all right. Cheap too. She's the kind that slips right through the cracks. See, nobody has the patience anymore. They want an instant racehorse. They don't see the potential. The long haul."

"Yeah, I guess."

"You gotta dig deep in this game. See the history behind it. The

cause and effect. The gold's right here, all you gotta do is dig for it."
He thumps the stack of catalogues again, sending more ash floating
up into the blue vapor. I resist an urge to go to him and pat him on
the shoulder, afraid he might react something like the way Rena
did. I would really like to pat him on the shoulder.

As I descend the stairs I hear the kids coming home from
school. The boy calling for his dog. The girl shouting good-bye to
her friends. The gate banging shut behind them. Their feet brushing through the fallen leaves. I'm full of fear. It's not just about how
I might find Rena in the kitchen; what state she might be in now. It's
not just about seeing his kids eye to eye; hearing them speak to
their mother; seeing their cold young breath in the room. It's about
the distance when I leave the yard. When I turn back on the street
and look up at his one window where the smoke is. About climbing
in my car to drive away. About leaving with no connection. How
there might not have ever been one to begin with. How there
might not ever be.

I'm crossing the kitchen as the kids bang through the back
door, letting all the dogs in. Rena's yelling: "Take your shoes off! I
just mopped the kitchen floor! Don't let those dogs in here!" She's
captured by her function; her motherhood; her basic survival kit. I
stop and stand there dumbly while the dogs crash around my
knees. Rena grabs one of them by the collar and starts dragging it
toward the back door to throw it out again; a squirming yellow dog
with a pink fluorescent collar. She looks back at me in the middle of
this with her hair flying wildly across her eyes. There's a whole different look in her face now. Fierce almost. "Well—" she says.
"What's the story? Did you talk to him?"

"Yeah. Yeah, I did." The kids are staring at me while they strip
their tennis shoes off and toss them into a basket full of hockey
sticks. Rena boots the dog out the back door and slams it. The girl

says: "Don't kick Tasha, Mom!" Rena says: "I didn't kick Tasha. I nudged her." The boy is eyeing me funny like I might be one of those dangerous compadres he's heard about from his father's mysterious past. "Did Dad come out of his room yet, Mom?" he says as he heads straight for the refrigerator, swings the door open, and stares at the orange juice. Rena doesn't answer him. She walks directly to me and stops, inches away from my face. I can feel her breath on my chest. She puts her hands on her hips and looks right into me. There's no hope in her face or anger or even fear. She just wants to hear what she already knows. She wants to hear me say it. "And?" she says. "Any news?"

"He said to tell you that one day he will reemerge. He will come back into the light of day." She drops her hands from her hips and turns to her daughter as though she hasn't even heard me. She smiles.

"How's my gorgeous girl?" she says, and sinks to her knees, arms outstretched to take the girl in. The boy slams the refrigerator door and doesn't move. His back is to me. He stays like that.

GREAT DREAM OF HEAVEN

A prideful thing had slowly grown between the two old men about who could rise earliest in the morning. Who knows where it got started. Sherman, the younger of the two by three years, had lately taken to sneaking out of his sleeping bag at 4:30 a.m. He would shuffle barefoot across the red linoleum in the pitch black, careful not to pick his heels up and cause any snapping sticky sounds. He would wrap a wash rag around the little chain switch on the fluorescent tube over the bathroom sink to muffle the hum as the light heated up and cast its flickering greenish gleam across the dreaming face of his partner Dean—his longtime partner, Dean. Sherman wasn't quite certain where this deep satisfaction of winning the "early riser" contest arose in him. There wasn't any money involved. No prizes of any kind. Most often they never even mentioned it to each other. In fact he couldn't remember if they'd actually formalized it into a legitimate competition. It had just evolved over the years out of their endless days and nights together. There was definitely a sensation of winning, though. That was unmistakable. Sometimes he felt it in his feet—a warmth ascending slowly up into the calves and behind his knees. Sometimes he felt it in his chest and arms—and one electric morning he felt it directly on the top of his head. His whole head lit up. He remembered that. It lit up much the same as the fluorescent tube above the bathroom sink—a bright glow that flooded through his skull, washed down into his neck and backbone, and then seemed to switch on a light through his entire body. It was a light he'd never known before, and the only comparison he could make was to a dream he'd had of heaven when he was about ten years old. In that dream a similar light had appeared and he remembered the sensation of being directly connected to some force as strong as the sun itself. For days, as a boy, he walked around with the memory of that dream in his head, but the light never appeared again until this business with Dean developed—years down the road—this unspoken rivalry about waking. Sherman's sense of victory was short-lived, though, since the very next morning Dean had managed to fake sleep altogether and was sitting ramrod straight, eyes wide open in the springback chair, while Sherman gurgled and buzzed away into his pillow. Dean had pulled the chair right up close to Sherman's mummy bag so there'd be no mistake on Sherman's part who the winner of the morning was. Dean could hardly wait for the sun to get high enough to warm Sherman's eyelids and cause them to crack. There he'd be, staring right down into his long face while Sherman struggled between some REM-dream and the realization that he'd lost. Dean watched Sherman's eyeballs roll and twitch behind the lids much the same as a dog's will. Even the little moans and whines that came out of Sherman's throat were similar to those of a sleeping dog. What in the world could he be dreaming about? Not women anymore—surely not that. Dean hoped it wasn't a dream about women. For Sherman's sake. They were both too old for that. Too painful. Why torture yourself when there were the simple pleasures of desert life to keep you company? The sounds of quail covied up in the shade; the smell of bacon, dominoes, spotting the mail truck's dust way off, miles away against the jagged shadow of Smith Mountain. But most of all, the one great daily pleasure they both looked forward to was their walk down to Denny's by the highway for coffee and paddy melts. That was truly like heaven to the both of them.

They'd known each other forever, these two. Grown up in the tiny South Dakota town of "Alma" (at least that's what the sign on the post office said). Went various separate ways over the years but always managed to reconvene until, finally, after separations and deaths of wives, and children moving off to silicon computer hell, they decided to share the same little cinder-block bungalow on the edge of Twentynine Palms. It suited them fine. They'd been living there, relatively content, for eleven years straight now. They'd had some minor ups and downs like the time Sherman found out that Dean had shot sixteen quail off the back porch with his 20-gauge and then had the nerve to cook up the breasts in a black skillet and serve the whole mess over scrambled eggs for breakfast. Sherman actually wept about the quail and Dean felt guilty for days, sitting in his rocker and realizing the deadly silence he'd caused around the bungalow. It took a full two weeks before the quail built up enough confidence to come back in and covey up with their soft, peaceful whistle again. By that time, Sherman had forgiven Dean and they were on to new and more exciting concerns—namely a waitress down at Denny's called Faye. One thing they both had an impeccable eye for was waitresses. Not just cute or sexy waitresses but waitresses with heart. Waitresses with the unmistakable stamp of compassion about them around the eyes. They were few and far between, they both agreed, but when they finally discovered Faye it seemed to fill them with new purpose. Each day at noon they would shower and shave, put on clean shirts, bolo ties, and their pressed khaki pants, don their "Open Road" Stetsons, then hike down the long dusty frontage road to the highway. Just before they entered the door of Denny's they would both rub the dust off their boots on their pant legs, check each other's tie for straightness, then remove their Stetsons and enter the air-conditioning. They were well aware of Faye's work hours and always arrived intentionally at the height of lunch hour so they could watch Faye in action. The two of them would stand patiently side by side with their hats held with both hands, covering their knees, waiting sometimes forty-five minutes for a booth, just to watch Faye swing her amazing hips through the kitchen doors, balancing trays of steaming turkey and BLTs and always with her heartbreaking smile sweeping across the multitudes: the fat, the ugly, the rude, the drunken, the insane—she made no distinction, they all received the same radiant beam of kindness from her eyes. Not that any of them recognized it and certainly none of them deserved it according to Dean and Sherman. The days of the "gentleman" were long dead but they made their appearance at Denny's each day at noon to remind Faye that her sort of beauty was a great blessing in the midst of all this sad madness. She appreciated it too. Her face always brightened a notch or two when she'd see them waiting there by the cashier, and the light would go on in Sherman's head and he even felt that maybe the same phenomenon was happening to Dean but he never mentioned it to him for fear Dean would think it too esoteric an observation. Dean liked things plain and simple. When they were finally shown to a booth they'd set their Stetsons side by side and upside down with the crowns resting on the shiny red Naugahyde upholstery. This was for good luck. If you set a hat with its brim down you'd never be able to catch any luck at all. They both knew that. And they both had a tacit understanding of how their version of "luck" had subtly changed over the years. It no longer had anything to do with money or success or health or the "future" of any kind—that was the main difference. "Luck" now had to do with the present. Sustaining the present. Celebrating it, in fact. To be sitting here now in this red booth with their backs to the plate-glass window and the Colorado River and the blistering Mojave heat—to be here in the icy breeze of the air-conditioning and to see Faye's eyes settle on them and smile that smile and head toward them with her pad and pencil ready to take their order—that was luck of the rarest kind. It was luck to have an enduring friendship, a true partnership, at their age and not be condemned to some horrible blithering sentence of aloneness in one of those glassed-in "homes" they'd pass now and then out near Palm Springs. There was no reason for either one of them to suspect that this lucky condition of theirs would ever change. They had no more expectations of life than this daily routine, this settled compact that the days and nights would be shared without complications, with not much talk and a deep sense of satisfaction at the smallest details like the way Faye would lick her pencil stub and make a little sigh. And this is the way things continued for Sherman and Dean well into their twelfth year in the cinder-block bungalow on the very edge of Twentynine Palms until one morning the sky completely collapsed. Sherman awoke slightly later than usual to find Dean gone. He searched the rooms, the porch, and the immediate area around the bungalow, making sure to take his hickory cane with him to ward off any rattlesnakes, but Dean was nowhere to be found. Sherman made himself a pot of sage tea and toasted a blueberry pop-up tart, then sat out on the porch with it, watching the rising sun transform all the colors of the yucca and manzanita. He watched a coyote slink across the dirt road with a pack rat in its mouth. He watched the heat vapors begin to rise in bands and get broader out where the asphalt highway begins. He listened to how the quail got quieter as the sun grew more intense and how the distant sounds of passing trucks became joined with sports cars coming in from L.A., racing toward golf and women and casino glitz. He had a short thought about his youth but shook it off. He knew where that would lead. He heard the tin roof on the porch start popping as it expanded from the sun's full glare and realized he'd been sitting out there in his rocker for well over six hours. Still no sign of Dean. It was now closing in on their time to go visit Faye down at Denny's so Sherman decided he might as well get himself ready, and by the time he was, Dean would have surely showed up. For some reason Sherman had trouble selecting a tie clasp for his bolo but he finally decided on the horseshoe silver-plated one with inlaid turquoise marking the nail holes. He decided on this one because it was the only tie clasp that Dean had an identical matching one of. They'd both bought them in a pawnshop over in Indio—again out of superstition that wearing them would sustain their good fortune. Sherman noticed that Dean's horseshoe was missing out of the box so he was surely wearing it, wherever he was, and if Sherman put his on that might help get them reunited. Sherman took his time getting into his khakis, his pressed shirt, and donning his "Open Road" but still Dean hadn't shown up and there was no sign of him down the long dirt road. Sherman started to wonder whether he shouldn't hike down to the root beer stand and make a phone call to the police— see if maybe there wasn't some report on Dean of some kind. Then he thought it was too soon for that, and besides, it was only inviting bad luck if you started looking for it. He waited five more minutes, standing squarely on the porch and squinting hard out toward the highway for the least trace of Dean's silhouette, but nothing appeared. Sherman strode off toward Denny's with a slightly sickening feeling rising up below his breastbone. It just didn't feel right walking alone toward Faye. There was an awful sense of betrayal about it even though he'd gone through all the waiting for Dean and looking all around the place. How would he feel if Dean had gone off to meet Faye without letting *him* know? Sherman stopped and turned around. He stared back at the bungalow—their bungalow. It looked emptier now. Emptier than it did when the two of them, walking side by side, would approach it after their long walks down to the post office or the grocery store or coming back from Denny's. Now it looked like it could be anybody's place. Sherman walked back up to the porch and went inside. He found a piece of scrap paper and wrote a note to Dean: "Where the Sam Hell have you gone off to? Meet me down at Denny's. I'll go ahead and order your paddy melt so don't dawdle. Sherman." He set the note in plain sight on the kitchen counter and placed their cactus-shaped saltshaker on top to anchor it. He looked across the kitchen for a second to the screen door as though half expecting to see Dean standing there, but he wasn't. It was a feeling like there might be a ghost present.

Down at Denny's Sherman waited by the cash register in the same spot he and Dean always waited. He stood the same way he would stand if Dean had been there right beside him, the brim of the Stetson lightly held in both hands directly in front of him. His spine ramrod straight, eyes searching for the first sign of Faye through the swinging kitchen doors. But Faye was not on duty this afternoon. He realized that after he'd already been seated in the red booth and another, younger woman with dark hair and a sour attitude came over to take his order.

"Where's Faye?" Sherman asked right off.

"Who's Faye?"

"You know, Faye— She's been working here for a year or more."

"I don't know any Faye," the dark-headed girl said, scribbling some number on her order pad and not looking up at Sherman's eyes.

"You don't know any Faye?"

"Yeah, that's right, I don't. I just started here."

"Well, where'd you come from?" Sherman said.

"What do you mean, where'd I come from? I applied for the job and they gave it to me."

"Well, where's Faye? What happened to Faye?"

"I don't— Look mister, I don't know anybody named Faye. I just started here today and I don't know anybody. All right?"

"Get me the manager. I want to see the manager."

"Oh boy— All right, look— Do you wanna order something first?"

"No, I don't want to order anything. I want to see the manager."

"You're not going to lodge a complaint about me, are you?"

"No. I just want to find out what happened to Faye."

"Because this is my first day on the job, and if you make a complaint about me, then—"

"I just want to know what happened to Faye! That's all! Where is Faye! Somebody has to know where Faye is!" Sherman slammed the tabletop with such force that the napkin dispenser flew off and struck the dark-haired waitress in the knee. When he sprang to her assistance the girl screamed in terror and the whole place froze. Now Sherman wondered if all his good luck had suddenly run dry. If now he would be plunged back into all the lost dark days before his peaceful life out here with Dean on the edge of Twenty-nine Palms. Back when he'd find himself waking up in ditches with broken ribs and his pockets ripped out. It could happen that fast. He knew it could. He'd seen it happen. Your luck just turned and that was it. Nothing much you could do about it. "Is there something I could do for you, sir?" The manager's voice came in a deep baritone. Sherman looked up to see a large smiling black man in a blue shirt and red tie. The dark-haired waitress girl was limping off into the kitchen whimpering about her knee.

"I was wondering what had become of Faye," Sherman said.

"Faye?"

"Yes, Faye. You know—the waitress. She's been working here every day for over a—"

"Yes, Faye. Certainly. I know who Faye is. She works here."

"That's right! She does. You know who I'm talking about."

"Yes, I do. What about her?"

"Where is she? Where is Faye?" Sherman heard the desperation in his own voice and it shocked him for a second. It shocked him to realize how much he depended on seeing her; knowing she was in the world at the same time every day.

"Well, she's been switched to the graveyard," the manager said.

"Graveyard?"

"Yeah, you know—midnight till eight in the morning. Grave-yard shift."

"Oh— So, you mean she still works here then? She still works here at Denny's?"

"Yessir—but she's on a different shift now. Nighttime."

"Oh— All right. I see."

"Was that all you wanted to know, sir? You weren't having any trouble with the new waitress, were you?"

"Oh, no—nothing like that. I just was wondering about Faye."

"All right, sir."

"Oh—there is one other thing."

"What's that, sir?"

"My partner—I come in here every day with my partner—Dean. You must've seen us. We always—"

"Oh, yessir. We know who y'all are. We recognize you."

"There you go— Well— You haven't seen him anytime down

here, have you? I mean—Dean—that's his name. You haven't seen him come in here at all recently, have you?"

"Oh, yessir. He was in just last night." Sherman felt something hit him between the shoulders like an electric jolt. At first he thought it might be his old bolt of light that he'd taken to be heaven-sent, but this was a sharper, more wounding kind of jolt like jealousy. That's exactly what it was—a jealous jolt right between the shoulder blades.

"Last night?" Sherman said in a short breath.

"That's right. He came in the wee wee hours—maybe three, four in the morning. Hardly a soul in here."

"Why would he do that?"

"Sorry, sir?"

"Oh, nothing—" Sherman said, and started to make his move to get up and leave the red booth. "You say, three, four in the morning he was in here, huh?"

"That's right. Musta been. Real late—or early, depending— They just sat over in the corner in that booth there, sippin' coffee and laughing almost till the sun came up." Sherman stopped and straightened his bolo. He stretched his neck as though trying to see right through the fireproof ceiling to the sky and then he placed the Stetson on his head. "There wasn't one customer to speak of so I just let her go ahead and visit. Couldn't see no harm in it. She sure is one grand lady, I'll tell you that much."

"She sure is." Sherman forced a smile and tipped his hat to the manager as he headed for the door.

Down the long dirt frontage road heading back to the bungalow Sherman had trouble remembering exactly where he was. For a while, he thought he might be back in Arizona working at the stockyards. He could smell the blood. He had to jerk his head up and stare at the horizon line to remind himself but he still didn't recognize the terrain. He hadn't had this panic of aloneness for a long, long time. The sun had reached that vertical zenith of the day when Sherman felt the back of his collar might actually catch fire. He adjusted his Stetson but the disadvantage of the "Open Road" in full sun was the short brim. His whole back seemed like it was blazing now and his head was like a steam kettle. He knew something was moving him but his mind wasn't able to fully connect with the pulse of his body. He watched the toes of his boots punching through the dust. He watched the cadence of his swinging arms but somehow felt outside the rhythm of it. As he approached the bungalow he caught a splinter of sun bouncing off Dean's matching horseshoe bolo. He saw Dean out on the porch sitting in the rocker, facing him. He knew it was Dean but he didn't say anything or even acknowledge him with a hand gesture. Dean didn't move either. He just sat there, stock-still, in the rocker facing out and silent. When Sherman walked right past him and went into the house Dean never moved an inch; just kept staring straight ahead. Dean could hear Sherman fishing around in the bedroom closet for something; opening and closing dresser drawers. None of the sounds Sherman was making had any anger about them or seemed intended to get a rise out of Dean. They just sounded like someone was in there looking for something or trying to sort things out. Finally Sherman came back out through the screen door with a small canvas duffel bag full of his things. The duffel had "U.S. ARMY" stamped on it in white by the broken zipper. In his other hand he carried a ukulele in a small green case with a piece of rope tied around it in a square knot. Sherman never paused or turned his head or made so much as a sound except for his boots crossing the porch and going down the stairs to the sand. Dean kept watching Sherman's sweat-stained back as he walked further and further away from him down the dirt frontage road. He kept an eye on the

X that Sherman's suspenders made between the shoulder blades. He watched the X get smaller. Suddenly Dean stood bolt upright from the rocker and walked right to the very edge of the porch and stopped dead still. His voice cracked a little as he yelled out to Sherman. It had been a long time since he'd yelled at anyone and his voice was a little shocked by it: "It wasn't my idea, it was *hers*!!" he yelled. Sherman never turned around. He just kept walking.

ALL THE TREES ARE NAKED

I find her downstairs, half asleep in an armchair, watching *The Third Man*. She's curled into her beautiful hips; really astounding hips that never fail to stir me. I slide my hand along her waist. She says "Hi honey" in a wistful little-girl voice. I sit on the arm of the chair and touch her bleached hair. "Isn't this a beautiful film?" she says as we watch the closing scene in black and white where Joseph Cotten passes Ingrid Bergman on the long country road and decides to get out of the jeep and wait for her.

"Look at those phony leaves falling in the foreground," I say. It just comes out of me. "All the trees are naked but there's leaves falling right in the foreground." She makes a hum of agreement and then I feel stupid for breaking the emotional spell of the film with a lame intellectual comment. Ingrid Bergman keeps walking toward the camera at the same steady pace. She has a great walk, full of female strength; tall, erect, and self-contained. Joseph Cotten lights his cigarette and waits. There's something arrogant about his waiting; something characteristically male. The leaves keep falling in the foreground, right in front of the lens. I start thinking about the hidden factors of filmmaking. The prop guys perched on tall ladders beside the camera, dropping autumn leaves so they float just right. The wind machine. Someone controlling the breeze. I've

140

just dropped into this. I have no connection to the story line or empathy with the characters. She's been watching from the start, in and out of sleep. Ingrid Bergman gets closer and passes Joseph Cotten without so much as a glance. She walks right past the camera, never changing her stride, and disappears, leaving him alone with his cigarette. His arrogance dissolves. He watches the path she's taken. There's a recognizable sense of loss and yearning in his eyes; those hound-dog eyes that seem like they'll never get the sleep they need. Suddenly I'm inside the film without quite knowing how I've been seduced. I'm caught right where the filmmaker wants me. The raw zither music is working on me. I believe the falling leaves are real. I make the leap of feeling toward the impossible gap between men and women. I'm feeling lucky to be here right now with the one I love, touching her bleached blond hair. The credits roll. "Why didn't Ingrid Bergman stop when she saw him waiting for her? She could see that he was waiting," I ask.

"That wasn't Ingrid Bergman," she says.

"It wasn't? It looked just like her."

"Well, it wasn't."

"Who was it then?"

"Someone who looks a lot like Ingrid Bergman."

"But it wasn't her?"

"No, it wasn't."

"Are you sure?"

"I'm positive."

"Well, why didn't she stop?"

"She blames him, I guess."

"Blames him for what?"

"Well, do you know the story?"

"It's been a long time. I guess I saw it in the sixties."

"She blames him for the death of Orson Welles."

"Oh."

"You remember."

"Yeah," I lie. I remember nothing about it except some kind of chase sequence through the sewers of Paris. Was it Paris?

"Don't you remember? They set him up. The vaccine?"

"Oh, yeah," I lie again.

"All those kids dying from the phony vaccine?"

"Right."

"Well, I'm totally exhausted. I'm going to bed. Can you lock up down here?" she says.

"Sure," I say. She leaves the room, yawning and stretching. I punch the remote control and the TV buzzes off to black. I watch the path she's taken. The sky lights up with sheet lightning through the big bay windows. I can see the river bright as day. Thunder rolls far off in the valley. It smells like rain and fish. The dogs scratch the screen door. They're all cowards when it comes to thunder. How long ago was it when I first kissed her and who was I pretending to be?

Sam Shepard is the Pulitzer Prize–winning author of more than forty-five plays as well as the story collection *Cruising Paradise* and two volumes of prose pieces, *Motel Chronicles* and *Hawk Moon*. As an actor he has appeared in more than twenty-five films, and he received an Oscar nomination in 1984 for his performance in *The Right Stuff*. His screenplay for *Paris, Texas* won the Golden Palm Award at the 1984 Cannes Film Festival, and he wrote and directed the film *Far North* in 1988. Shepard's plays, eleven of which have won Obie Awards, include *Buried Child, The Late Henry Moss, Simpatico, Curse of the Starving Class, True West, Fool for Love,* and *A Lie of the Mind,* which won a New York Drama Desk Award. A member of the American Academy of Arts and Letters, Shepard received the Gold Medal for Drama from the Academy in 1992, and in 1994 he was inducted into the Theatre Hall of Fame. He lives in Minnesota.

A NOTE ON THE TYPE

This book was set in Monotype Dante, a typeface designed by Giovanni Mardersteig (1892–1977). Conceived as a private type for the Officina Bodoni in Verona, Italy, Dante was originally cut only for hand composition by Charles Malin, the famous Parisian punch cutter, between 1946 and 1952. Its first use was in an edition of Boccaccio's *Trattatello in laude di Dante* that appeared in 1954. The Monotype Corporation's version of Dante followed in 1957. Although modeled on the Aldine type used for Pietro Cardinal Bembo's treatise *De Aetna* in 1495, Dante is a thoroughly modern interpretation of the venerable face.

Composed by Creative Graphics, Allentown, Pennsylvania
Printed and bound by R. R. Donnelley, Harrisonburg, Virginia
Designed by Soonyoung Kwon